CHAPTER ONE

In which Teddy commentates a sport... ...lum in Shropshire, and Stilts Sto... ...se.

"WAGS WIPPLE still le... ...final straight, but Bluebottle is n... ...while Plodder stakes his place on

Now it's Wags Wipp... ...Wags Wipple, Wags Wipple... Bluebottle is within reach but now it's Fleet Flat Feet stealing the inside.

They're at the distance but it's not over yet as Copper Buttons bursts into second place with a daring carpe diem up the middle giving Fleet Flat Feet a chronic case of fourth place.

Copper Buttons and Bluebottle are neck and neck and closing fast on Wags Wipple. Wags Wipple eyes the enclosure as he approaches the final furlong and this race is his to lose — oh, no, and that's just what he's done. Wags Wipple has hopped the fence..."

Theodora 'Teddy' Quillfeather, who had been commentating the event from a raised vantage point on the steps of the Shaftesbury fountain in Piccadilly Circus, lowered her opera glasses.

"Wags has crashed into the terrace of the Criterion." Teddy resumed binocking and her coverage of the race. "He's knocked over three tables, an ice bucket, and what looks like either a vice-admiral or a concierge."

"The home straight has always been his weak suit." Frederica 'Freddy' Hannibal-Pool, Teddy's co-conspirator and trainer of record to recent favourite Walter 'Wags' Wipple, topped up their champagne glasses. "Same thing happened last year, and the year before that he'd have taken the 1926 Saint-Martin-in-the-Field to Westminster Steeplechase by a walking two lengths if he hadn't hurdled the rail at embankment and landed up in the river."

The sport of provoking London policemen into a flat mile-and-a-half occupies, at best, a grey area of British law. Mindful of this, Freddy and Teddy maintained a perforce low profile among the flaneurs and flappers profiting from a warm spring afternoon and the hospitality of the steps of the Shaftesbury fountain. Both were in the uniform of late-twenties girls in their late-twenties, including the latest in shapeless shimmy dresses and feathery headgear. Freddy tamed her blonde mane in French braids and Teddy opted for the iconic brunette bob. They might have been any of the dozens of innocent Londoners, although they were the only two with champagne and binoculars.

Teddy raised a stand-by hand. "Don't tear up your betting slip yet, Fredds..." She squinted into her spyglass. "Here's a turnip of a turn up — the rozzers have nicked the wrong wag. Looks like they've pinched... yes, that's Crib Digby. Fancy both he and Wags Wipple wearing green damask swallowtails."

"Has Wags still got a chance to make the finish line?"

"Hard to say. The Criterion terrace is manifesting a very fine example of the best kind of chaos." Teddy panned the racecourse. "And we have a late entry, ladies and gentlemen — a sergeant no less, just rounding the final turn at Coventry Street and going well. Blimey — a five-constable foot-chase just for one helmet."

"Has Wags still got it?"

"Not if he has any intelligence he hasn't." Teddy returned her surveillance to the terrace. "So, yes, of course he's still got it. He's hiding it under his coat and cantering casually this way while Copper Buttons, Bluebottle, Plodder, and Fleet Flat Feet search the terrace and generally harass a very astonished Cribbage Digby."

"What's become of the sergeant?"

"Ehm..." Teddy scanned the Royal Enclosure. "No sign of him. Here's Wags, though. What ho, Wags."

"What ho, ladies." Wags, as mentioned, was a young London gad in green damask swallowtails, under which he secreted a policeman's helmet, which he now produced at what would shortly prove to be an ill-chosen moment. "Got it."

"And I, son, have got you." The then-to-fore invisible sergeant simultaneously appeared and spoke this clever if somewhat derivative quip, and assumed possession of a fistful of green damask collar. He was an economy-sized sergeant with a military bearing and whiskers like an old-growth Leyland cypress, and he

Frauds On Favourite

The Second Teddy Quillfeather Mystery

Frauds On Favourite

presented as a decidedly by-the-book sort of rozzer, with little use for the beat cop's discretionary mercy. His buttons glimmered and his uniform was trim but, notably, incomplete — he was missing his helmet.

"Oh, what good fortune." Teddy put her opera glasses behind her back. "Here's a policeman now, Wags. Wags was just telling us, sergeant, that he found this constable's helmet and he was asking what we thought ought be done about it."

"We suggested that the right thing to do was to find a policeman and turn it in," confirmed Freddy. "Isn't that right, Wags?"

Wags, picking up instantly on the proposed stratagem, said, "I didn't pinch it."

"Oh ho?" enquired the sergeant.

"Ho!" replied Teddy and Freddy in unison.

"We'll sort it all out down the nick," said the sergeant, adding, "No thank you miss, not while I'm on duty," in response to Freddy offering him a glass of champagne.

"Nick, sergeant?" Teddy furrowed an innocent brow. "What's a nick?"

"Bow Street Magistrates, as I expect you very well know, young lady." The sergeant levelled on Teddy the squint of the street-hardened peeler. "In point of fact, Miss, don't I recognise you from a raid on an illegal Soho nightclub only Friday last?"

"You most certainly do not," said Teddy with cold confidence, for on that occasion she had been dressed like a gondolier and her face was painted blue. Her own mother wouldn't have recognised her. "Tell me, sergeant, what goes on at this mick of yours?"

"Nick," corrected the sergeant. "You will appear before a magistrate and you will be required to give your name and address, and then you will be given a trial date on which you will answer charges of creating a disturbance and making illegal book on an equally unauthorised sporting event."

"My name?"

❦

3

"Tilly Fivequidder." Teddy repeated this subtle perjury the following morning, complementary to explaining her presence on a rain-slick train platform in Shropshire. "So I thought I'd see in the start of Flat season a safe distance from the metropolis."

"Very wise, Teddy." Tilden 'Stilts' Stollery, who had come to collect Teddy at the station, thought everything she did and said was the very tipping point of top drawer. "And you can't get much safer or more distant than Market Middleditch. What fate faces Tilly Fivequidder, should she ever have her day in court?"

"Going by personal precedent, probably five days or a twenty pound fine," estimated Teddy. "The case for the crown, I'm afraid, is air-tight, but Tilly has one of those faces that brings out the grandpa in most magistrates."

"I'll say she has." Stilts cocked his head to the side in the manner employed to famous effect by Yorkshire Terriers. The effort was almost entirely wasted, though, because Stilts is taller than Teddy by two and a half tophats and — not atypical of his self-awareness — he wore a tophat. He also wore black swallowtails fitted to his flagstaff frame and the supervening effect was less Yorkshire Terrier and more giraffe mortician. "Dashed class clash of haps, isn't it, you and me being at your uncle's estate at the same time? There's a vicar on hand too, if you can possibly believe it. Rather makes one think the circs are trying to tell us something."

"I was thinking that very thing..." Teddy was dressed more in keeping with the drizzle and draft in a royal blue trench coat and matching slope-brimmed fedora, "...but remember what happened last time we impersonated the Bishop of Willesden and his wife. I'm still not convinced those children are technically baptised."

"I meant that we should seize the opportunity, as it were, and get married."

"To whom?"

"Each other."

"You think the fates want us to be married?" doubted Teddy. "They obviously don't, Stilts. If the fates thought we ought to be married they'd have made us twenty years older. You know I'm too young to take on the care of anything taller than a three-inch heel."

"You're nearly thirty, Teddy."

"Why, that's absolutely uncanny, Stilts," marvelled Teddy. "If you said that as though you had a migraine coming on you'd sound exactly like my mother. Where's the car?"

"At Middleditch." Stilts referred, for the record, to Middleditch Castle, Shropshire country seat of Lord Markham Quillfeather. "Your uncle let me take the carriage."

Stilts tipped his hat towards the little brick ticket office of Middleditch station, beyond which stretched a mosaic of fields and pastures in the muddy, ruddy browns and bogs that characterise the end of winter soaking into Shropshire. Not contrasting with this in the slightest were the sandstone, rust-toned ramparts of Middleditch Castle, huddling beneath the drizzle and mist. A road of sodden soil curved in and out of view behind conifer copses and farmhouses, across stone bridges over rushing waters and under dripping elm bowers, eventually rolling up at Middleditch station with a two-wheeled covered carriage harnessed to a tawny trotter, who gazed calm curiosity at Teddy with big brown eyes.

"Why didn't you bring the car, Stilts?"

"I've just said, Tedds, your uncle let me have the carriage." Stilts picked up Teddy's two travel bags. "I'm hardly going to pass up a chance to drive a horse, am I." He stalked like a careful crane down the slippy steps to the road. "In any case, the Bentley sank into the drive before I could get halfway to the gatehouse. Took two Shires to pull it out."

"What, by the by, brings you to Middleditch, Stilts?" asked Teddy as the carriage came about with a dash and a splash of runny road.

"I've just told you, Teddy — fate brought us together." Stilts leaned forward to say to the horse something that sounded, to Teddy, like 'Hi ya!'. "However, lending destiny a hand was your uncle, who invited me up for unofficial Flat season."

"There's an unofficial flat racing season?" Teddy neatly dodged a knob of mud kicked up by the horse. "When does it start?"

"Last Monday."

"That's the first race of the official season, Stilts," Teddy pointed out. "The Lincoln Handicap. I was there. So were you."

"I refer to the Middleditch flat racing season." Stilts subtly but meaningfully jostled the right rein, keeping the horse tight to a road that intersected no others, following a route he'd trotted a thousand times, on several occasions alone or with a sleeping driver.

"This village has its own flat racing season?" Teddy referred as it passed to the scattered, soaked, honeysuckle cottages, hostelry pubs, post office, newsagent, covered market, and wide array of equestrian kitters-out that comprised the town of Middleditch.

"No, Middleditch Castle has its own flat racing season," specified Stilts. "Also National Hunt, but it starts and ends a week after the official one, such as to allow time to install the hurdles and sober up the jockeys. It's all strictly off the books and it's run at the racecourse on the estate. This afternoon's card is a cracker-jack, incidentally — Greengrocer's Eight Furlong for Fillies Under Two Years, Saint Paul's and All Angels Choir Handicap, and Middleditch Bridge and Backgammon Club Apprentice Four Circuits for Colts and Fillies with Unshorn Tails, to name but three."

"But Uncle Markham is so wholly horsey, how can he possibly bear not running any of his stable in the legitimate race calendar?"

"Well, obviously, Teddy, he does." Stilts recovered his topper, which had been knocked off by a positive beamer of a clump of mud. He put it back on his head and it was immediately knocked off again. "The unofficial races are experience for untried under-two-year-olds. The rest of the stable is fully engaged in the purse races across the nation, not to mention Deauville."

Stilts raised a 'just-a-second-while-I-focus' finger. He leaned almost imperceptibly to the left and squinted at the sloppy road ahead. After a moment of cold calculation he flicked the left rein and relaxed the right in a considered manoeuvre that was entirely ignored by the horse.

"Point of fact, Tedds, the official season is why your uncle really invited me up." Stilts assumed a serious tone and, very briefly, took his eyes off the road ahead. "There's been a spot of trouble."

"A spot?"

"I say a spot." Stilts looked down at a shirtfront so specked with mud as to be mostly mud, and gave further consideration to the word 'spot'. "Spill might be more accurate, at the risk of sounding pedantic. Or possibly deluge?"

"Uncle Markham has had a deluge of trouble?"

"Yes." Stilts nodded decisively. "Deluge is definitely the word. He's at risk of being warned off."

"Warned off?" Aghast, Teddy only by a hair evaded two hoof-sized lumps of sopping Shropshire topsoil, going about sixty miles an hour. "But Uncle Markham and Aunty Lew love racing. They positively live for it."

"Nevertheless..." Stilts seemed to come to the light himself, in that moment, and briefly allowed the horse a free rein. "...unless something is done, Lord and Lady Markham and their entire stable will be banned from racing for cheating."

"What utter tosh," Teddy called it. "Uncle Markham would never fiddle a horse race."

CHAPTER TWO

In which Lord Markham fiddles a horse race.

"I FIDDLED A HORSE RACE."

Teddy's Uncle Markham made this claim against expectations from a puddle. Markham Lord Middleditch wouldn't be remarkably tall standing on a marble plinth, and so he was compelled to look some distance up at Teddy from the depths of one of the many puddles that ornamented the path from Middleditch Castle to the estate racecourse. This particular model came to the very rim of his Wellington boots. From there up Lord Markham was in patched and repatched tweed mucking (demoted from gardening) trousers, followed by a hunting jacket formed of two previously unrelated hunting jackets and elbows from a saddle blanket, topped by a favoured cloth cap held together largely by sentiment and protecting a mainly bald head above a winsomely shaved, cherubic and apparently deceptively innocent face.

Teddy and Stilts, unlike Lord Markham, had not wandered absent-mindedly off the stone path, and hence they stood, respectively, above His Lordship and way above His Lordship.

"I don't believe it for a single second," estimated Teddy. "You'd never cheat. Not at the races, at any rate. You cheat at cards all the time but you're so bad at it that it doesn't count."

Lord Markham lowered his gaze to the mud, such that Teddy could see his bald spot through his hat.

"And yet, I'm afraid it's so, Theodora." He looked up, newly inspired. "Not just the one time, either. I'm a serial cheat."

"No, you're not." Teddy corrected. "I thought we were going to look at the horses."

"I appear to be stuck." Lord Markham examined his puddle. "You children go on ahead. Have fun."

"Pull him out, Stilts." Teddy stepped aside with a sigh.

"On three, Your Lordship. One, two, three — alley..." Stilts, bending almost double, took Lord Markham's hands. "...oops."

Lord Markham, perhaps predictably, now stood on the flagstone steps in mismatched socks darned with mismatched yarn.

"Thank you, Tilden." Lord Markham continued up the steps.

"But, Your Lordship, your boots…"

"Marshpool will collect them." Lord Markham smiled vacantly at his boots, one of which was sinking. "He always does."

The stone steps arced up the hill to a plateau and the answer to an historic mystery.

Soon after Middleditch Castle was built in the thirteenth century it became known as Hidey Hall. It wasn't called that — the Plantagenet loyalists who built it named it Hide Hall after the 'hide', a measure of land upon which most taxation was based. It was initially employed by the notoriously high-maintenance administration of Edward I as a way station for his beloved taxes, such that they might have a little rest along the trying journey to London.

Over the years the castle was abandoned and reoccupied and abandoned again and, for most of the 16th century, it served as a hermitage for a breakaway coenobium of brothers who had taken a vow of poor hygiene. Once again, it was abandoned and then awarded by Elizabeth I to Sir Guy Montbrume on his elevation to the First Duke of Broom, in consideration of some perceived sleight at court.

The Third Duke of Broom abandoned the castle sometime in the early 1600s and this time it took. Hidey Hall remained an uninhabited but richly productive mushroom plantation until 1842 when Gilbert Quillfeather, made viscount in exchange for keeping quiet about something, acquired the castle and the village of Middleditch. The First Viscount Middleditch spent a fortune restoring the castle and, very soon, discovering not only the origin of the name Hidey Hall but the reason it had been so frequently and enthusiastically abandoned.

Middleditch stables and racecourse occupy a broad, flat hilltop on a direct eyeline to the tallest tower. For nearly seven hundred years, the grounds of Middleditch Castle have been sinking, relative to the surrounding hills. Now the ramparts peek shyly over the castle's own lawns and gardens, explaining the affectionate epithet 'Hidey Hall', and its status as England's most vexing drainage problem explain why no one wanted to live there for very long.

Apart from occupying what amounts to a trench, the castle is a comfortable clutter of old stone and modern home, with multiple guest rooms and dining rooms and games rooms and reading rooms and rooms the purpose of which has been long forgotten. With the addition of a wooden footbridge the first floor had become the effective ground floor, and the ground floor an effective sluice over, it is strongly suspected, a subterranean river. This theory gained considerable authority, recently, when an engraved, leather-bound agenda that Lord Markham dropped in the buttery was found three months later by a mudlarker under Blackfriars Bridge.

The grounds at that time of year were saturated and a menace to boots and Bentleys but were nevertheless a delightful tangle of sovereign hedges of primula candelabra, scruffy, independent gatherings of great burnet, liberty-loving lobelias, giant, headstrong rhubarb, wild, willful willows, and several cypress trees with subversive leanings.

Picking its way through this harmonious disarray was an equally random and randomly overlapping network of paths, laid over the centuries in gravel here and flagstone there, the steps of an old oak staircase, and rude rock. The more recent pathway climbed the hill to the driest and most valuable land in the entirety of Middleditch, and it was reserved for the horses.

Teddy, Lord Markham, and Stilts looked, respectively, over, under, and down from above the white lathed fences of Middleditch Castle Racecourse. Surrounding the track and carpeting the enclosure was clipped and green turf, and the course itself was a hand-balanced surface of oak bark and fine gravel. Topiaried poplars bordered the paddock on the other side of the course and then again to shade the newly whitewashed stable buildings. Above, the sun carved a little gateway through the grey.

Presently, a coffee-coloured comet blurred past in a whir of thud and thunder.

"Oh, jolly good," cheered Stilts as they watched the horse and his rider — who appeared to be performing the largely incidental role of hanging on for dear life — already on the turn. At distance, objects in motion appear slower, even when that motion is whip-snippy, and so the flurry clarified briefly into a palomino with a snow-white mane and tail and, under this rare ray of direct sunlight, specks of gold in his café-au-lait coat. He moved like a Swiss timepiece built for performance and he did so at the speed of thought, and indeed by the moment that Teddy had formed these impressions he was once again hurtling past.

"Chockit Rockit." Stilts put a name to the marvel with a tone of unworldly awe. "The most beautiful thing I've seen since picking you up at the station, Tedds."

"It *is* a lovely station," agreed Teddy. "Hallo, Mister Yardpole!"

Teddy waved at the compact, cable knitted, stable kitted trainer in the enclosure, spinning in circles as he endeavoured to follow Chockit Rockit's progress. He tried gamely to return the wave but, very apparently very dizzy, he just kept turning.

"Is this whish the work of Mister Yardpole?" wondered Teddy. "Lovely chap, but it was my impression that his training strategy featured a very prominent element of chance."

"I think the horses just like him." Stilts watched Mister Yardpole endeavour to treat his vertigo by turning slowly in the other direction. "He had two plate finishers and a derby winner last Flat season, and seven top finishers in the National Hunt, but over both racing seasons he lost three."

"Three's not a lot of races to lose," pointed out Teddy.

"He lost three horses, Tedds," clarified Stilts. "Good ones, too. We suspect he got to talking to the queen and was too embarrassed to own up to training the horses that had just left hers looking like portraits at the post."

"Bringing us back to Chockit Rockit — how has Mister Yardpole managed that?"

Teddy nodded to the whir as it welted by, during which the jockey made a sort of "...eeeeeeAOoooooo..." sound.

"Well, that's the mystery, isn't it?"

Throughout this exchange Lord Markham had been moaning softly and gently knocking his head against a fence rail, in aid of which he had removed his hat.

"It's no mystery..." His Lordship raised a despairing dial to Teddy. "It's my doing. I did it with my violin."

Teddy looked to Stilts for a translation into Sane.

Stilts smiled indulgently. "Your uncle believes this remarkable performance is a direct result of playing Chockit Rockit selections of jazz violin."

"Irish reels," corrected Lord Markham with a slow, dismal shake of the head. "I knew I was playing with fire."

"Quite right, Irish reels. Chockit Rockit has the speed and endurance of a youthful comet because Lord Markham plays him Irish reels on his violin."

"Not really," doubted Teddy.

"No, not really."

"Yes, really." Lord Markham assumed a feverish, earnest tone, and then lowered his voice. "It's how I fiddled Chockit Rockit's last race."

"That's not what fiddling a race means, Your Uncleship," said Teddy.

"I mean that's how I cheated."

"You see, prior to striking upon the winning formula of the Irish reel played amateurishly on violin," explained Stilts, "Lord Markham had been experimenting with Baroque, Romantic, and... was it Gershwin, Your Lordship?"

"Dixieland," moaned Lord Markham. "And nothing took."

"Just a tick, Uncle Muncle," Teddy held up a tick-finger, "what made you think that Chockit Rockit would run faster on any violin music at all?"

"Ah." Lord Markham nodded with a sagacity that ill-suited his dress and demeanour and widely-held reputation. "It's a proven, scientific method, Teddy. Chockit Rockit performed exceptionally in training and had a record-breaking season opener."

"Because you were playing him your violin," concluded, dubiously, Teddy.

"Just so." Markham nodded with a donnish reserve. "Science."

"Or, playing the devil's advocate," considered Teddy, "coincidence."

His Lordship put an analytical hand to pensive stubble. A mere minute of this produced solid results, "Well, I had to be sure, didn't I? In the interests of science."

"Right, science," conceded Teddy. "Why didn't you just keep playing whatever it is you'd been playing before the season started, then?"

"Excellent point, Teddy," acknowledged Markham. "I forgot."

"You forgot what you'd been playing."

"I didn't realise that the extraordinary speed improvement was so closely related to genre, at the time," confessed Markham. "So I didn't make note of what I'd been playing, only that Chockit Rockit instantly began performing poorly, starting with Bach's *Chaconne.*"

"That is something of a yawn in D minor," observed Teddy. "Mama used to play it on the phonograph at the end of a whisk night to remind everyone to go home, but the vicar kept falling asleep on the spot."

"Nothing else worked either, though." His Lordship watched Chockit Rockit canter to a bouncy halt on the other side of the course. "He had a terrible season, until, on a whim, I played him *The Wind that Shakes the Barley.* He was like a different horse. And then with *Tam Lin, The Maid Behind the Bar,* and *Drowsy Maggie,* he went from strength to strength until, finally..." Lord Markham completed the dire confession in a choking whisper, *"...Dunmore Lasses."*

"This was the eve of the Cheveley Handicap at Newmarket," added Stilts. "Chockit Rockit's seventh race of the season — seventh sanctioned race ever, in point of fact — after five dismal showings, including a Chiswick Bell from which he was disqualified for hopping the fence and cutting across the Tattersalls Enclosure."

"And then came the Cheveley Handicap," lamented Lord Markham.

"Did it in a walk," coloured in Stilts. "The next quickest horse was six full lengths behind him, and he came in second by an easy four lengths."

"Hence the suggestion of cheating," reasoned Teddy. "Anything to it, do you think?"

"I've just told you," moaned His Lordship, "there very much is something to it — *Dunmore Lasses.*"

"Anything rational, I should have said," clarified Teddy. "Stilts?"

"I mean to say, it was an extraordinary improvement." Stilts gazed back at the horse. The jockey had dismounted and he and Mister Yardpole were helping one another to stand. "So it doesn't much matter how it happened, it's certainly being received by the racing community as shifty as an eight-gear two-seater."

"What does Mister Yardpole say?"

"Rather a lot of things about the 1902 Epsom Derby, if you give him half a chance," recalled Stilts vaguely. "It's a bit of a trial keeping him focused. He has a tremendous number of draws on his time as trainer and racecourse manager."

"What does he think of the violin theory?"

"Obviously, Teddy, I haven't told him," disdained Lord Markham. "No one outside the household knows what I've done."

"Sound policy, Uncle Mark — what if it was to be discovered, against all odds, that Irish fiddle music can't, after all, completely transform a horse, then you'd look a right thimble-wit." Teddy scanned the gleaming stables which occupied, along with a weighing room and jockey lockey, the horizon. "How many resident horses are there, when it comes to it?"

"Ninety-one," replied Stilts. "Quite light, in fact, and getting lighter. During the overlap between National Hunt and Flat season there can be over two hundred."

"And Mister Yardpole trains them all?" boggled Teddy.

"Oh-my-dear-light-beer no," staggered Stilts. "He only trains the Middleditch stable. The rest are boarders with their own trainers. That's still some dozen horses, mind you, for Mister Yardpole to personally tutor in the poetry of the pace."

"Just a tick..." Teddy returned her attention to Stilts. "Did you say the population of horses on hand was getting lighter?"

"I did say that, yes."

"Why?"

"Because it's getting lighter," elucidated Stilts.

"Quite. Why?"

"There's going to be a stewards' inquiry." Stilts spoke as one pointing out the obvious. Lord Markham groaned and found a despondent manner in which to put on his hat.

"A stewards' inquiry?" asked Teddy. "Just for one astonishing win?"

"One astonishing win preceded by five sitting losses," Stilts reminded the court. "Chockit Rockit started the Cheveley Handicap at a nearly unprecedented eighty-to-one. Some shrewd shonk positively cleaned up when he came in six lengths ahead of the next nearest hopeful."

"And the Jockey Club thinks that Uncle Markham is the shonk in question."

"Stands to reason," said Stilts. "It's been suggested that Chockit Rockit was held back, somehow, in a deliberate attempt to drive up the odds."

"Well, what if he was?" Teddy wanted to know. "It's not illegal, is it?"

"It's worse than illegal, Tedds — it's against Jockey Club rules, and it can get a chap and even an entire stable warned off."

Once again, Lord Markham dug deep to register anguish and, without knowing it, reproduced to a slim nicety the reaction of Burbage's Romeo on discovering what he thought to be Juliet in death.

"But you don't bet on your own horses, do you, Uncle Marks?" asked Teddy somewhat leadingly.

"No, of course I don't," protested His Lordship. "That doesn't change the fact that I cheated, though. I'll be warned off. I'll lose the stable. Your aunt will probably leave me for a chap who's not been warned off and I, of course, will have to wish her well. It's all I deserve."

"And, as mentioned, some horses have already been withdrawn," said Stilts. "No one wants to be associated with a stable when it's struck off."

"Is that a real possibility?" asked Teddy.

Stilts issued a gallic shrug. "It was Lord Bitterbrook who raised the objection, and he carries rather a lot of weight with the Jockey Club, not to mention many of the owners. He started the stampede by withdrawing his best horses from Middleditch, including Maid of Money, a very winny steeple-chaser who, as a young filly, presented the unique training challenge of refusing hurdles if they weren't high enough — Overdraught, double cousin to Chockit Rockit and, I'm told, an exceptional hurdler in his own right — and Cheque Mate, a very clever cuddy on the flats and the second-place finisher from the aforementioned Cheveley Handicap, where all the trouble started."

"So unless it can be shown how Chockit Rockit demonstrated impossible improvement without cheating..." Teddy began to summarise.

"...which I did," added, unhelpfully, Uncle Markham.

"...which you obviously did not," continued Teddy, "then the entire Middleditch stable will be banned from racing, ruining the estate and the economy of the entire town, and denying all Quillfeathers, including me, access to the enclosure of every racecourse in England. Does that about capture the gravity of the situation, Stilts?"

"In a nutshell." Stilts nodded gamely at Chockit Rockit as he pranced about, apparently anxious for another go around. Then the penny and his face dropped in unison. "Blimey, Teddy, something must be done."

CHAPTER THREE

In which it is recounted how King Waffles got his name, Teddy takes drastic measures, and the stewards take a firm hand.

"THERE'S NOTHING TO BE DONE."

Stanley Lord Bitterbrook, who Teddy had provisionally identified as the villain of the affair, was a guest at Middleditch Castle. This entitled him to the lush hospitality of Lord Markham's table, enforced by decorum and the obligations of aristocracy, and kippers. Teddy found him, accordingly, at a sideboard that ran the entire length of the mediaeval dining room and creaked under the obligations of aristocracy, including the aforementioned kippers, chafing dishes of fried eggs, scrambled eggs, poached eggs, and hard-boiled eggs, racks of hard toast and pots of butter, cream, jam, and marmalade, plates of ham, bacon, and sausages, pans of asparagus, French beans, and mushy peas, black pudding, bread and butter pudding, and rice pudding, and so on off into the distance, halting only when it came to a thick stone wall with floor-to-distant-ceiling lancet windows looking out onto a lush green ditch.

"Oh, do come along, Bitters. Papa always goes on about how kind and generous and reasonable and, oh, let's say, wise you are." Teddy had joined the breakfast rush soon after returning from the tour of the racecourse but had taken the trouble to swap out her train togs for a rainy-day twill.

"It was your father that gave me the name Sticky when we were at Eton." Lord Bitterbrook — Sticky, to Teddy's father and everyone else who'd known him since fourth form — was the result of years of enthusiastic appreciation of other people's sideboards and, combined with a testament to tailoring wizardry in brown tweed, he presented not unlike an upholstered barrel. He also wore an ascot that he had been compelled to borrow from the Earl of Kettleby at Christmas, a goldfinch waistcoat that he had so far neglected to return to his brother-in-law, and dress Balmorals that Marshpool, Middleditch Castle butler, had loaned him on arrival. Through handsome gold pince-nez — which had become his principle pair since discovering that he and Lord Markham share the same strong reading prescription — he examined his plate for remaining space.

"Well, there you go then..." Teddy took up a pudding bowl and filled it with black coffee from a clay urn. "Papa doesn't just distribute nicknames to those for whom he has no regard. It was he who first called King George 'Waffles', you know. And His Majesty loves it — uses it to sign all acts of parliament."

"It's out of my hands, Teddy..." Sticky wavered between the roast potatoes and the rissoles, but the battle was brief and he soon surrendered to both. "I have no influence with the Jockey Club — I'm only able to raise an objection, like anyone else."

"Lower it again, then, Sticky," suggested Teddy from behind a two-handed coffee bowl. "You know Uncle Marky would never cheat."

"I know no such thing." His plate full, Sticky stuck a handful of cheese straws in his pocket, wrapped in a kerchief he found in the library. "I do know, however, that after five finishes in which I could have beaten him myself, on foot, Markham's Chockit Rockit somehow found the form to give my own Cheque Mate six lengths worth of dust."

"Yes, I know." Teddy swirled her coffee with a dismissive air. "He told me all about that. It was nerves. Chockit Rockit was intimidated by the crowds but then, at the Cheveley Handicap, under the calming eye of Lord Bitterbrook, he just came into his own."

"I was not present," disdained Lord Markham. "I was at a claim race in Deauville."

"You were there in spirit," shifted Teddy. "Handily represented by Cheque Mate. It made all the difference in the world to poor Chockit — you know how skittish thoroughbreds can be. So glad we cleared that up."

"I thought Markham was maintaining that it was a freak fiddling accident."

"Not at all," scoffed Teddy. "That's just a story being put about by his enemies, to make him look foolish."

"I'm not withdrawing the objection, Teddy."

"Very well, then, Lord Sticky-Bitter, then I'm not

withdrawing the rumour I'm starting about you and a certain chorus girl who goes by the name of Lavish Lee."

With sad resignation, Lord Bitterbrook scanned the tremendous length of the wax-worn dining table, now hosting little cliques of guests. "No one would believe it, I'm afraid."

"No, I daresay you're right." Teddy followed Sticky to two oak-and-velvet thrones, and she plucked a kipper from his plate.

"There are plenty more on the sideboard, Teddy."

"You know, I'm not sure there are," Teddy deftly nicked a rasher of bacon. "Are you in training for something? A sumo match?"

"Your charm offensive, in case you wish to know, Theodora, is failing to win me over."

"At least keep your horses at Middleditch stable."

"I am keeping some horses at Middleditch stable." Lord Sticky shifted his plate to a protective siding. "I'm only moving the best of them. I can't risk having them here should the stable be warned off."

"Oh, I say — I know how you could eliminate that risk altogether." Teddy held up a victorious kipper.

"I'm not withdrawing the objection."

"Quite sure?"

"Quite."

"Then I must warn you, Lord Bicky, that I'm prepared to take drastic action." Teddy snapped to her feet.

"I don't doubt it."

"Starting with..." Teddy dodged for another kipper, Lord Bitterbrook parried, Teddy thrust and pinched, "...this scone," and she marched down the dining hall, without looking back, to take drastic action.

"Good morning, Lady Bitterbrook."

"Good morning, Teddy." Lady Olivia Bitterbrook, unlike her husband, wore only her own clothes and she didn't even wear them for very long. This morning she was airing a radical departure from the stovepipe winter season in the form of a *Jane Régny* double-breasted black blazer and diagonal skirt that was still warm from the Paris runway.

"What ho, Lady Lulu."

Across from Lady Bitterbrook sat Llewella Lady Middleditch.

She was dressed similarly to Lady Bitterbrook, because when she came down for breakfast and spotted her childhood friend and school-days idol dressed for lunch at *Le Grand Ecart* with Harry Cahill, she went back to her room to change out of the riding habit she wore on race days and into a tailored tweed ensemble, and then from that into a chantilly tea dress, followed (very briefly) by a rhubarb ball gown with red piping and puff shoulders, and finally back to the tweeds judging, and very much throwing caution to the wind, that this was as close as she was going to get.

"Good morning, Teddy. I'm so very glad you were able to break away from the city and join us."

"Yes, very sweet of you." Lady Bitterbrook glanced over her teacup at Teddy's twill rigging. "I see you didn't even take the time to pack. Have you nothing you could let Teddy wear, Llewella?" She appraised Lady Llew's tailored tweeds. "Anything new, I mean."

"No, I know, I look a state." Teddy looked down at her outfit. "I took this off a scarecrow. Gave him my *Jane Régny* skirt suit in exchange. Lady Lulu, are you aware that you nourish a viper in your bosom?"

Lady Llewella laughed a disengaged, whimsical, please-stop-noticing-me laugh, and waved her fork in a manner intended to be casually dismissive but instead launched a morsel of kipper across the room.

"I'm not sure that I know what it is to which you refer, Teddy."

"Lord Bittysticker has raised an objection to the results of the Cheveley Handicap, the inquiry into which could well see Uncle Markham, you, Middleditch Stable, and even me, warned off all racecourses in England," explained Teddy. "*And* he's hogged all the bacon."

Lady Llewella spoke directly and clearly to her plate. "That's just the boys being mischievous, Teddy. It's all in good fun." She looked up at Lady Bitterbrook. "Do you recall how we used to tease one another at school, Olivia?"

"No."

Lady Llewella concluded, somehow, that the best reply to this was a giddy laugh. When she was done, she confided to Teddy,

"She's such a card…," and then asked Lady Olivia, "Do you remember locking me out of Hyde Abbey overnight in just a swimming costume?"

"Was that you?" Olivia Bitterbrook deigned to furrow half a brow. "Are you quite sure?"

"Once, she organised all the other girls — and some of the mistresses — to pretend to have forgotten my name for an entire term," Llew reminisced to Teddy adding, in a trailing note, "We still laugh about it."

"I knew a girl like that when I was at school," said Teddy with happy harkening. "At least, she was like that until she was dyed green in a freak bath mishap."

"How extraordinary."

"Thank you."

"I'm so pleased you'll both be here for today's second race." Lulu set aside her plate and enthused over a teacup. "Spoons is running his first Middleditch match."

"A horse, I trust," ventured Teddy.

"A direct descendent and the unerring image, in appearance and attitude, to Elmer, the horse I had as a little girl." Lulu stirred her tea absently and gazed up and away into a sweet so-long-ago. Then she looked into her tea and saw there something sad. "Elmer is no longer with us."

"Do pull yourself together, Lew," advised Lady Olivia.

"Quite right. Sorry." Lady Llewella tried and failed to pull herself entirely together. "It took years to track down the lineage but wait till you see him run — he's such a perfect bouncy ball, just like his great-grandfather. Oh, Vicar!" Lady Lulu chirruped and waved her fingers at a living advertisement for Cleric and Country. "I saved you a spot."

"Sit here, Vicar," invited Lady Olivia. "The sun won't be in your eyes."

"Sit here, Vicar," countered Lady Lew. "The sun will be on your face. Teddy, you know Reverend Bittles."

The Reverend Bittles, whom Teddy did not know, sat next to Lady Middleditch but across from Lady Bitterbrook, balancing a diplomatic quandary, a plate of toast and marmalade, and the trying task of being young and handsome in the morning.

"What ho, Vicar." Teddy poured him a cup of tea. "Have you

got a minute to excommunicate someone for me?"

Reverend Linus Bittles smiled a warm, comforting smile, a smile that, were it a pudding, would be Yorkshire. The vicar wore vicar's vestments — the backwards collar and black shirt — under a herringbone coat that showed exactly the wear a coat gets from helping parishioners repair their roofs and look for their cats in the rain. He had clear, rosy cheeks and a head of happy, chestnut curls, and yet, somehow, a manner and demeanour that betrayed a good hundred years of patient ministering.

"We don't really do much excommunicating in the Anglican church, Miss…"

"Quillfeather," provided Teddy. "Not even for a chap baldly bearing false witness? I'd say you have a practically airtight case of coveting his neighbour's donkey, too. Almost literally."

"Then I think I can do better than excommunication, Miss Quillfeather," proposed Vicar Bittles. "This Sunday, I shall preach the parable of Zacchaeus the Tax Collector."

"Yes, that should do it," considered Teddy. "In the meantime, Lady Bitterbrook, can I trust you to get Sticky to withdraw his objection with the Jockey Club about the ethics of the man with whose bread and kippers you are currently bursting?"

"I do wish you wouldn't call him Sticky, Teddy."

"No, I know, and I agree with you Lady Bitterbrook," said Teddy, "but there's a vicar present."

"I never meddle in Stanley's affairs."

"You never meddle in his affairs?" reprised Teddy. "As recently as this month, according to the papers, you made him buy Golden Acres."

"I mean to say, I never involve myself in his racing interests."

"Golden Acres is a horse."

"Surely, Teddy, you're not suggesting that the affair be covered up." Lady Bitterbrook delivered this mainly as a performance for Vicar Bittles, who smiled handsomely in reply.

"No, I'm suggesting that there's no affair to cover up."

"Then that will doubtless be the finding of the inquiry, but I couldn't possibly be seen to interfere." Lady Bitterbrook idly and unnecessarily adjusted the pin in a *Maison Reboux* pillbox hat, so fresh from Paris it still smelled of cigarettes. "Appearances are everything."

On the sunny Shangri-La that was the flats and rolling greens of Middleditch Stable Hill, an invasion of sorts had been mounted. The town residents who, indirectly or otherwise, owed their livelihoods to Middleditch Stable, milled to the edges of the parade grounds, paddock, and enclosure, transformed from stock villagers to clowns, fortune-tellers, pantomime horses, pirates, piemen, and tea ladies, or the farmers, greengrocers, publicans, and shopkeepers that they were when the day started, but wearing their wedding-and-funeral suits, church frocks, home-made fascinators, and wellies. This was the closest that most of them would ever get to Royal Ascot and it was, in the main, close enough.

The air was a swaying overlaying of springtime and stables and wet grass and damp earth and woodsmoke, and it rang with children's laughter and adults' laughter and hawkers and tinny tannoy announcements for the last race and the next.

Teddy wandered the festive village fête, immersed in the buoyant community atmosphere and momentous anticipation and absence of policemen who knew her face. She'd been to Royal Ascot but on balance preferred the sincere will to have honest fun of Middleditch's unsanctioned race days, and would have preferred them a great deal more were it not for the oppressive omnipresent probability that this was the last of them. The dark irony, as Teddy saw it, was that cheating among stables amounted to the very wealthy stealing trifles from one another, and it probably happened all the time at every stable except this one.

Presently, Teddy's path crossed that of a small horse who seemed to be working its way through to the refreshment stand. This horse caught Teddy's attention partially because it was wearing a homburg with a daisy in the band, and partially because when it saw her it stopped, looked furtively about, and then whispered,

"Be mindful with your money, Teddy — there's all manner of fraud at Middleditch Stables."

CHAPTER FOUR

Featuring proud Spoons, suspect tunes, and blameless balloons.

"AUNTY AZALEA?"

Teddy recognised the horse's voice as that of her maiden aunt, Azalea Boisjoly. "Why are you a pantomime horse?"

Aunty Azalea is of a highly introverted nature. She almost never leaves her home in rural Hertfordshire and never receives guests who aren't family and even then she dines in her room. Only the month prior to the events described herein, she finally agreed to have a telephone installed in her house so that her butler, Puckeridge, could more quickly and efficiently tell callers that she wasn't at home.

In short, anyone who could have known Azalea Boisjoly at all well would have known, too, that what Teddy meant when she asked 'Why are you a pantomime horse?' was '...as opposed to, say, a fern?'

"Because no one ever wants to talk to a horse," replied Azalea in the tone of homespun counsel.

Teddy stepped back to survey the horse which, in addition to a homburg with a daisy in the band, was wearing polka-dotted overalls.

"Who's the back end?"

"I'm not sure..." whispered Azalea, "...we haven't been introduced."

Teddy, too, lowered her voice to a conspiratorial hush.

"You know about the cheating?"

"I do," Azalea replied, hoarsely.

"Have you worked out how it was done?"

The horse's head nodded gravely. "The coconuts are nailed to the post."

"Coconuts?"

"Nailed down." The horse once again searched the crowd for spies. "But this is the clever bit — not all of them."

"How does nailing down coconuts make Chockit Rockit suddenly fast?"

"I very much doubt that it would."

"Then to what fraud do you refer, Aunty A?"

"The coconut shy," explained Azalea. "It's impossible. Don't waste your money."

"You played the coconut shy?" marvelled Teddy.

"No, of course not," scoffed Azalea. "My findings are the result of close observation."

"Have you observed anything else unusual, Aunts?"

"The pluck-a-duck fishing lines are elastic."

"Anything to do with the stables, I mean," specified Teddy. "Such as would explain Chockit Rockit's astounding performance at the Cheveley Handicap."

"Oh, yes, everyone's talking about it," whispered Azalea. "You'd be surprised what people are prepared to discuss in the presence of a pantomime horse. It's a very effective disguise."

"What are people saying?"

"That Lord Markham cheated."

"Well, he didn't. How are they saying he did it?"

"He told his jockeys to hold Chockit Rockit back — start late, deliberately get boxed in or drift to the outside — until the Cheveley Handicap."

"I see." Teddy considered this catastrophic development. "And who's your source for this?"

"Oh, everyone." Azalea waved an expansive hoof. "The tea ladies favour the jockey theory, but you should know there's a not insignificant minority of the drainage guild who hold the view that Lord Markham upset Chockit Rockit's training regime by postponing vital culvert maintenance on Middleditch racecourse."

"Talking of Middleditch racecourse, what brings you up to Shropshire?"

"The races. Lady Markham invited me."

"Odd she didn't mention that you were here."

"I haven't actually seen her yet." Azalea scraped idly at the turf with her hoof. "I had Marshpool put me in the north tower."

"Isn't the north tower closed?"

The horse nodded. "There was a mudslide. Most fortuitous."

"Well, Lulu will be looking forward to settling you in properly.

When did you arrive?"

"A week ago," said Azalea. "I didn't want to be a bother."

"What ho, Teddy." Stilts, his top hat schooning above the throng like a mast, hove through the crowd. "Who's your friend?"

"Whinny," said Azalea, as though reading it as it was written.

"Pleasure's all mine, I'm sure, Winney. Got any stable-talk tips for us?"

"Neigh."

"Right oh," accepted Stilts in the sporting spirit. "Shall we go through to the enclosure, Tedds? I've saved us a spot at the finishing post."

Stilts and Teddy crossed the crunchy gallop to the inner circle and to a choice standing prospect held in trust by a silk-suited sample of the class system.

"James Fairleigh, Theodora Quillfeather," presented Stilts. "Teddy, James."

Teddy took in the James Fairleigh experience the way one takes in a department store Christmas tree. This particular spectacle was formed of cultivated grey at the temples, precision-shaved features, and a monocle. He was expertly tailored into his race-day swallowtails, complete with gaiters, lapel carnation, ruby cravat pin, and mallard-head brolly. The only imperfection was his bowtie, which had a slightly descendent leaf, and that, of course, had been deliberate.

James Fairleigh appraised Teddy and spoke with the diction for which Oxford holds a royal warrant, "You are most decidedly not Lord Markham's daughter. I've met the man. You'd be a hand shorter and built more for endurance over hard terrain."

"His Lordship is my first cousin, once removed," confirmed Teddy. "However, as a girl, my mother once ran from Chipping Wolc to Ascot during the spring thaw just to rescind a birthday party invite."

"James knows everything there is to know about racing," enthused Stilts, "and then some."

"I thought you knew everything there was to know about racing, Stilts," said Teddy.

"Didn't say I didn't, Tedds, but James takes what you might call the mathematical view." Stilts leaned on the fence in a manner seemingly contrived to give James the floor. "Tell Teddy what you were saying about Lord Markham's unique situation, in re Chockit Rockit."

"Bang to rights."

"Steady on, Mister Fairleigh," advised Teddy. "They haven't even convened the inquiry yet."

"Bang to Rights is a horse, Teddy." Stilts, endeavouring to twirl his top hat, dropped it.

"And a most gifted hurdler..." Fairleigh continued the narrative.

"...she'd clear hedge, ditch, post, and rail like you'd step over a crack in the pavement, Teddy," colour-commented Stilts.

"Just so," agreed Fairleigh. "And this remarkable talent earned Sinjin Lord Ashby's paddock 5,000 pounds in honest purse money, from her breaking maiden season in 1925 through to the end of the 1926 National Hunt, including a very respectable place in that year's Grand National."

"But then..." foreshadowed Stilts.

Fairleigh: "Then she dropped to a limping last place in every race in which she was run."

Stilts: "Got so bad she was very nearly disqualified."

Fairleigh: "But then..."

Stilts: "But then, with a now barely-deserved starting price of forty-to-one, she flew over Plumpton to take the Ovingdean Handicap Chase by five-and-a-half comfortable lengths."

Fairleigh: "There was an investigation, of course..."

Stilts: "...and in fact it was Sinjin Lord Ashby himself who raised the objection..."

Fairleigh: "...concerned, he claimed, with appearances. They can often be quite shallow, the privileged classes..."

Stilts: "We're a bad lot."

Fairleigh: "It was brought to the attention of the stewards that Bang to Rights' uncanny decline coincided with the introduction of the very latest in amusements for those who dislike the races but for some reason go to them anyway — helium-filled balloons."

Stilts: "Bang to Rights was afraid of balloons, and who wouldn't be? These red and green orbs, floating all over the shop, they put her off her game. But Plumpton Racecourse..."

Fairleigh: "Plumpton didn't yet have balloons, and so there was no obstacle to Bang to Rights returning to her previous spectacular form for the Ovingdean Handicap."

Teddy surveyed Stilts and Fairleigh with a sceptical finger to a cynical chin.

"Balloons."

"Those were the official findings..." stated Stilts.

"...of the stewards inquiry," finished Fairleigh.

"Is it true?"

"No," said Fairleigh, with the monotone of casual expertise. "What never came to light..."

Stilts: "...although we knew it..."

Fairleigh: "...is that Sinjin Lord Ashby owns and operates the balloon concession at all English racecourses. The other aspect of the affair which was never presented to the inquiry..."

Stilts: "...which, again, we knew..."

Fairleigh: "...was that Lord Ashby was instructing his jockeys to hold back Bang to Rights, coincidental with the release of balloons, giving his horse a plausible excuse for hobbling through half-a-season..."

"...setting longer and longer odds on Bang until Sinjin Lord Ashby was able to ruin his booky in the Ovingdean Handicap Chase," summed up Stilts.

"But, why?" wondered Teddy. "Why nobble his own horse if she was bringing home such rich purses?"

"The most mundane and obvious reason in the world, Miss Quillfeather," Fairleigh assured her.

"Income tax," furnished Stilts. "Roughly nine shillings on every pound for a two-fisted tycoon like Ashby."

"But there is no tax on gambling winnings," furnished Fairleigh.

"Nor, notably, is there a limit," added Stilts.

"So Sinjin Lord Ashby got ahead of the inevitable objection by raising it himself," recapped Teddy, "and distracted the inquiry with balloons."

Fairleigh gazed distractedly through brass-and-leather-bound binoculars. "Spoons."

"You said balloons, earlier," Teddy reminded him. "If possible, spoons makes even less sense."

"Spoons is a horse, Tedds." Stilts inclined inklingly towards the parade paddock.

The entrants in the auspicious Middleditch Guild of Navvies and Drainage Workers Twelve Furlong Plate for Untried Two-Year-Olds gathered in an excitable mottle. Of the six adolescent, wide-eyed colts and fillies prancing in the paddock, only one was very likely to answer to the name of Spoons. This was a chestnut redhead with a happy, hoppy disposition and ears the rough size and shape of basting ladles. Further setting himself apart from the herd, Spoons had a chicken on his head.

Spoons was a young horse with little life experience and, compounding this characteristic neither ill nor hale, was a comparatively short attention span. He didn't know that he was about to participate in a race and, if asked his views on the matter, would have smiled and nodded. He had already forgotten how it was he'd arrived in the paddock and was in fact largely indifferent to the point. This was a horse who lived in the moment, and in this moment he knew and only cared to know that he was surrounded by good mates and being cheered by a crowd of friendly strangers and he knew as well as he knew anything (which, while not a strong endorsement, was enough for him) that everyone was admiring his chicken.

Spoons was neither modest nor vain — he was a horse — he was, however, a little cockily aware that he was the only horse in the paddock with a chicken on his head, and that furthermore it was a very, very fine chicken. It was a snow-white hen that he'd known forever, so far as he could recall, and of all the horses in the stable she had deigned to ride on his — and only his — head. This comprised, in the moment, Spoons' entire world view.

The chicken, in so far as Spoons had ever heard her called anything, was called Chicken. She was a Leghorn of calm and regular habits and her sentiments regarding the state of affairs almost exactly mirrored those of Spoons. In a perfectly balanced emotional symbiosis she, too, felt honoured that she was riding the finest horse in the stable (which to her, incidentally, were all the horses in the world).

Now the atmosphere altered in a manner that put Spoons in mind of another thing that he very much enjoyed. He couldn't recall what it was and in fact he made no effort to do so, but he associated it with the fiddly stable lad who secured a saddle to him, and then helped the little fellow with the sing-songy voice into said saddle. And now the little fellow was gently handing Chicken down to the stable lad, for her part in the proceedings, Spoons vaguely recalled, was perforce that of spectator.

Now Spoons had five of his best mates in the world on either side and he looked excitedly about and danced behind the cord. Now the cord fell and Spoons forgot everything but the instant — he was thundering with his herd, hooves rumbling a rolling rhythm on the grip as they swept in a wave across the grassy savannah.

Horses don't know they're in a race, obviously. If they did, most of them would be appalled. However some have a notion of contributing to the herd by running on ahead, and Spoons felt uniquely qualified because a) he knew the way and b) he was the one with a chicken. And so he ran on ahead, a bit, keeping one of his giant ears attuned to the fading sound of trailing hoofbeats. The chap with the sing-songy voice — whom Spoons just then remembered was on his back — seemed pleased with the view, and in the blur of friendly, shouty strangers Spoons spotted Chicken, under the arm of Woolly Man. He gave a winning whinny, and whisked past the post.

"Sixth long lengths over twelve furlongs," marvelled Stilts.

"Six and a short head." Fairleigh watched Spoons prance happily sideways across the track to reunite with Chicken. "It'll be more — a good deal more — when he learns to focus."

"Direct descendent of riding school favourite Elmer, I understand," contributed Teddy. "Gifted stepper-over of brooks with an unparalleled capacity for avoiding steep inclines, and famous for doing tricks for strawberries."

"I think it likely Spoons will outshine even that sterling record," estimated Stilts. "You'll want to get your money down just as soon as he's put up for an official meet."

James shook his head. "Too late for that already. He'll be odds on favourite starting any race for which he meets conditions."

Teddy reflected on the value of this intelligence before proposing, "I won't tell if you don't."

"Word has a way of getting out." James raised his binoculars to follow Spoons as he pranced a majestic victory lap with Chicken on his head. "And I understand he'll be running several more Middleditch races first."

"Spoon's reputation will outrun even him, what?" mused Stilts.

"Assuming he runs at all," said Teddy. "Lady Llewella is awfully fond of him."

Stilts waved at Chicken as they cantered past. "Of course he'll run. A horse's first sanctioned race is like a girl's debutante ball. Would you have wanted to miss your Queen Charlotte?"

Teddy nodded with conviction. "Not for the world. It's terribly character-building, you know. You find you draw upon previously unsounded reserves of poise when presented to the king and queen with squeaky-toys in your shoes."

"Well, there you go," said Stilts without, clearly, thinking it through. "It's the same for a thoroughbred. A horse doesn't have a name, officially, or a stable, for that matter, until he's registered for his first sanctioned race."

"It would be a crime against the sport to not race such a horse," James judged.

"So long as there's no question of violins," hoped Teddy.

"Violins?"

"Hm? No, not violins. Balloons. I said balloons."

"Poppycock."

"Well, that's my story and I stand by it."

"Poppycock is a horse, Tedds," said Stilts, "and the dire moral of the story of the balloons."

"Poppycock's owner is Sir Benedict Babbacombe." James polished the lenses of his binoculars with a white silk fogle that he kept in a tortoise-shell case. "Sir Benedict was a clubmate of Lord Ashby, and privy to the balloon ruse."

"And, as chance would have it, Sir Benedict was also around that time particularly fascinated by the idea of not giving half his winnings to the exchequer," added Stilts.

"He didn't claim that Poppycock was afraid of balloons," ghasted Teddy.

"Nabucco." James tucked his binoculars into a matching brass and Moroccan leather case and closed the clasp.

"Another horse?"

"Opera by Verdi," said Stilts. "Scarlet Darby Babbacombe is Sir Benedict's better half and amateur opera fly-half and, according to evidence set before the stewards' inquiry,

Poppycock's largely winning performance was owed to easy afternoons on the gallops with Lady Scarlet and Verdi."

'Until Scarlet developed a case of laryngitis which lasted from the Newmarket Town Plate until The Oaks..." James deftly swapped his racing cravat pin for a simple silver socialising stud.

'...by which time Poppycock was lucky to get twenty-to-one, and then..." continued Stilts.

'...Lady Scarlet's laryngitis cleared up," James added the expected.

'Did the Jockey Club buy the story a second time?" Teddy wanted to know.

"They most thoroughly and spectacularly did not," Stilts assured her. "You see, by the time Sir Benedict got round to trying it on with the Jockey Club, they'd already worked out that the balloon wheeze was just that."

"Sir Benedict Babbacombe was warned off, never again to be seen on hallowed grounds." James put his hand to his heart and profited from the moment to smoothen a satin lapel. "The trick can never be made to work again, and anyone trying it would be guaranteed to be banned for life."

"Even if, speaking purely hypothetically," whimsied Teddy, "the stable in question was that of a known eccentric?"

"I doubt very much that would have any bearing," judged Fairleigh. "Sir Benedict was known to follow Lady Scarlet on her outings, providing accompaniment on a cabriolet constructed of two wheels and a kettle drum."

"Pish, that's nothing," waved away Teddy. "I've got a first cousin once removed who serenades his horses with a violin, an aunt who wears a disguise to dinner, even when she's dining alone, and an uncle who announces all evening meals with a live cannon, which he insists on loading and firing himself."

"How is Lord Stibling?" asked Stilts.

'Recovering nicely, thanks."

'Right then, shall we be getting our betting boots on before the next race?" enthused Stilts.

'Betting on unsanctioned races is quite entirely illegal, Tilden," James reminded him. "Let us hope for Lord Markham's sake that he's not allowing any gambling at Middleditch races."

CHAPTER FIVE

In which Teddy doesn't meet a leg man who offers no odds on the fourth race, and Mister Yardpole loses count of all the hats.

"WOULD YOU CREDIT IT, MADAM — I hear there's gambling going on at Middleditch races."

This scandalous scuttlebut was shared in a nudge and a whisper by a freckle-faced boy of about fourteen, dressed somewhat unnervingly like a grown man in a navy-blue blazer and trousers, soft-collared shirt and a tie in electric blue and orange, and a pocket triangle. He had been loitering in the line for the tea ladies' tent behind Teddy when the outrage became too much for him to contain.

"Shocking." Teddy took in the boy, who casually rocked on his heels and professionally scanned the crowd. "And what do these rumours say about the odds on the next fixture?"

"The Middleditch Lawn Bowling Club Open Eight Furlongs," said the boy with the aplomb and accent of the urban urchin who's made his own way in the world. "Six through at five-to-two, all bar two, joint favourites at two-to-one Mind If I Do and Dumb Bell, starting prices only." He stepped forward to keep pace with the queue. "Is what I've overheard. Shameful, I calls it."

"Tell me, ehm…"

"Richard Purdy, madam," said Richard Purdy. "'Me intimates call me Chard."

"Right, tell me, Chard, can you introduce me to the chap for whom you're legging?"

As Teddy had surmised, Chard was a leg man for an established bookmaker. Leg men are the sales representatives of the bookmaking trade, identifying and selling and upselling favourable odds and fairplay or, at any rate, the appearance thereof, to racing enthusiasts who may or may not have come to the track that day with the fixed intention of laying a bet. A certain tactful diplomacy is a core qualification for a good leg man, particularly at events at which trackside betting is strictly forbidden by law.

For his age, Chard was a top-notch leg man, prized for his discretion, his eye for the flush punter, and his trade experience. Indeed, Chard's navy-blue suit was a slightly modified school uniform that he took off a boarding boy from nearby Picklescott College in an ad-hoc conkers tourney and his tie — in the orange and blue of Bun Hill School for Boys — was similarly acquired. The pocket triangle was an expertly folded page of *Track and Turf.*

"Oh, with the greatest of pleasure." Chard nodded enthusiastically. "But would Madam not like me to fetch a constable, first, to ensure clear communication of the facts?"

"I like you," said Teddy sincerely. "You are a leg man, though."

"Not as I am willing to admit, madam, no," claimed Chard. "But if you was to flatter me with your confidence such as to trust me with your stake, I believe that I might by pure chance run into the gentleman what is the subject of these scurrilous rumours."

"Right oh." Teddy withdrew two pound notes and eyed the talent gathering in the paddock. "Any of them catching your eye?"

"Very difficult to assess form, madam, at these regionals, but number four, Mind If I Do, is attracting the confidence of the dab punter, and I wouldn't die of surprise if his odds were to shorten to three-to-two before starter's orders."

During this exchange, Teddy and Chard had allowed others to pass and they now constituted the entire queue to the tea tent, wherein five interchangeable apple-faced old ladies stood behind linen covered card tables at their posts of cake, cookies, biscuits, buns and tea, smiling hopefully. Leaving the tent at that same instant was Vicar Bittles with Lady Llewella and Lady Olivia on either arm, very much in the fashion of a professional-class tug o' war.

"What ho, ladies, Vicar," greeted Teddy. "You know Chard, of course."

Lady Llewella and Lady Olivia indicated that no, they did not know Chard, and intimated that they had no burning desire to make his acquaintance. Vicar Bittles, however, knew Chard.

"And what laws of Lord and man are you breaking even as we speak, young Richard?"

"Oh, none at all, Vicar," claimed Chard. "I mainly come for

the ginger cakes and Punch and Judy but then, what a treat, turns out there are races."

The vicar settled a kindly, country, clerical countenance on the boy.

"Bury your worthy nature as deep as you wish, young Richard — it will only grow that much stronger and sturdier and selfless when it comes into the light." The vicar's eyes twinkled, his cheeks dimpled, and, somewhere, a bell tinkled.

"My very words to the lads at bible club last night, Vicar, where I sometimes give of my time to help out the younger boys with some of the trickier parables."

Vicar Bittles received this venial sin with an indulgent smile.

"There'll be a performance of *Jerusalem* before The Saint Paul's and All Angels Choir Twelve Furlongs. I trust we'll see you there."

"Wouldn't miss it for a double-serving of ginger cake, Vicar."

Vicar Bittles and his admirers departed, and Chard smiled after them, writing out Teddy's betting slip.

"I always like to share this recipe of my dear old mum's," said Chard as he wrote, "for Third Course Pudding — two pounds of flour, a first-choice egg beat with four ounces of sherry, serves two-to-one."

Teddy paid two pounds for the recipe.

"Mum also does a lovely Fourth Fixture Custard," offered Chard.

"I'll have a butcher's at the candidates, first, and make a pick by the finalé of *Jerusalem,*" said Teddy.

"With regrets, I will be unable to attend the performance of *Jerusalem,*" regretted Chard. "You see, it's not so long ago I was a member of The Saint Paul's and All Angels Boys Choir, and the memory still chafes, not a little. I find meself particularly chivvied by a tenor solo."

"Then why did you leave?"

"I was the subject of a bidding war between Saint Paul's and All Angels and Saint-Martin-in-the-Fields, which turned quite ugly, and put me off the whole wheeze, if I'm honest."

"But you're not honest, are you Chard?"

"In point of fact, it was Vicar Bittles what thought I ought make a spot for a younger boy, who might better profit from the experience, and who wasn't organising games of Pontoon at a penny a hand in the parish clerk's office," reminisced Chard. "It's my own view, in light of the number and age of other lads also scratched from the running, that the vicar's chief reasoning was that we was getting bigger but the cassocks was remaining the same size."

"One outgrows things," sympathised Teddy. "It's why I had to give up the Bugatti."

"A right apt comparison, madam. Same story, really, but for one or two particulars."

"And that's when you became a legger, is it?" asked Teddy.

"Might have been, if I was a legger, but I ain't, so no."

"Right, well, if you were, would you have noticed any particular rise in interest in a horse called Chockit Rockit leading up to the Cheveley Handicap at Newmarket?"

"Eighty-to-one..." Chard took on as dreamy a look as one with his cynical outlook can. "And even at them extended odds, there was very few takers, owing to, going by Chockit Rockit's five races prior to the Cheveley Handicap, his retirement from the sport."

"Ah ha..." Teddy received this, erroneously as it will be shortly seen, as good news. "There can't be any question of cheating, then, if no one really profited from the stretched odds."

"I'd be inclined to agree with that view, madam, if it had a half-an-ounce of sense, but I never said that no one bet on Chockit Rockit, only that there was very few takers. Very few is a bit more than none at all, in the mathematics of odds-making, and even if I was working for a bookmaker, which of course I ain't, I feel quite sure that he's one of many with whom bets might have been placed."

"Yes, good point, well made," agreed Teddy. "All right then, who was it who won big on Chockit Rockit's triumph at Newmarket?"

"You'd be very surprised, I'm sure madam, at how few of my off-track regulars would thank me for telling their tales to everyone who asks." Chard shook his head in disbelief. "I've offered to give a full accounting of their daring and enterprise to the newspapers, but they're too shy. Let someone else have the spotlight, they all seem to say. It's my conviction that a natural-born modesty is the principle common characteristic shared by the habitual punter."

"Let's make it five quid, shall we?"

"That's very generous, madam, but could you advise me on a practical point — if you was to put yourself in a position that required retiring in anonymity to foreign parts, how would you best do that for five pounds?"

"Tell me this much and I'll take five pounds on the slowest horse in the fourth race." Teddy withdrew five one pound notes from her opera clutch. "Did Lord Markham bet on his own horse?"

"No madam." Chard accepted the notes. "To my knowledge, His Lordship doesn't bet on any horses, but I can add this for nothing and for sure — somebody knew for a fact that Chockit Rockit was going to win the Cheveley Handicap."

❦

"Nobody knew that Chockit Rockit was going to win the Cheveley Handicap."

Mister Yardpole's assertion presented as good if not better than any opportunity to mention that it was wrong. The lifelong stable lad, stable hand, farrier's apprentice, stable hand, veterinary apprentice, stable hand, bloodstock apprentice, stable hand, trainer's apprentice, stable hand, trainer's apprentice and then, finally, trainer, knew horses. He knew horses and Middleditch stables and most of the racecourses in England and eight words of French, acquired from accompanying Middleditch entries to the *Grand Prix de Deauville* and which he usually managed to work into most conversations. What Mister Yardpole did not know, in addition to wine, the first thing about home economics, his father, and the current prime minister, was people, and his contention that no one knew that Chockit Rockit was going to win the Cheveley Handicap was firmly founded in the fact that he didn't know that, either.

"I know people," said Mister Yardpole, neatly illustrating the above, "and nobody would nobble no horse of that quality just to make a few quid. It would be *days-honour-awble.*"

Teddy levelled an indulgent smile on the simple soul in thin cable knit, thin hair, and thick sideburns planted in deep Wellies.

"Why else would anyone nobble a horse, Mister Yardpole?"

Teddy had joined the Middleditch doyen at the edges of the paddock parade, where together they admired the lineup of lineage queuing to run in the hotly contested Lawn Bowling Club Open Eight Furlongs.

'Oh, now, there, Miss Quillfeather, you open an entirely different sack of oats." The trainer nodded with a world-weary cynicism. "I once knew a bloke back in '92 – or were it '93? Oh, no, I remember, it were the Easter Trial Stakes last month at Cheltenham – Sir Percy Pershore told his jockey to finish behind a promising maiden mare called Madam. Madam finished first and Sir Percy's horse, After You Madam, came second by a short head."

"He nobbled his own horse for the sake of a joke?" asked Teddy. "I believe I could find a friend in Sir Percy."

"No Miss. You see, Madam was from the personal stable of Her Majesty, Queen Mary. Sir Percy nobbled his own horse as a matter of *no-bless oh-bleeje.*"

"What a pillock."

"Just as you say, Miss."

Presently, Spoons pranced by, head held high. To look at his casual gait one would think that he didn't even know he had a chicken on his head.

"Is there anything exceptional about Spoons, in your view, Mister Yardpole?" asked Teddy.

"There most certainly is, Miss." Yardpole nodded warmly at his charge. "He's very quick out of the gate, for such an inexperienced flatter. Got an instinct to him that's a rare thing to see."

"I was referring to the chicken."

"Atypical," agreed Mister Yardpole, "but not unheard of. We had another two-year-old roan colt here in '18, called Strawberry... no, it were a three-year-old bay mare called Juror Number Thirteen, and it were 1919... or were it 1920?" He snapped his fingers, soundlessly. "No, it were 1922 – I remember, because that was the year we had a rose grey filly named Sprinkles who wouldn't enter the paddock without her straw hat."

"Sprinkles made friends with a straw hat?"

"Not as such." Yardpole crossed his arms and nodded sympathetically into the past. "It would be more faithful to the facts of the affair to say that she developed an attachment to straw hats, as a species. She loved her hat, you see, but once in the parade paddock she'd tip it off and eat it, and then after the race she'd pine for her hat with such feeling it made a man sad to witness."

"What did you do?"

"We give her another hat," replied Mister Yardpole. "Weren't even a very similar hat, every time, neither, but Sprinkles, while a lovely hurdler on dry ground, had all the brains God give a shoe tack."

"How many of Spoons' chickens have suffered unfortunate basting accidents?"

"He's only ever had the one chicken." Yardpole watched Chicken duck her head as she passed beneath the door of the stable. "Which is a very lucky thing, too — you see, hats and chickens can be very different animals, sometimes. It's a simple thing, taking an example to hand, to train a hat to stay on a horse's head, but it's not a practice that comes very natural to a chicken."

"You're not saying that you trained a chicken."

"A much more challenging undertaking than you'd think."

"I'll bet it isn't."

"They're prey to what you might call a disordered mind, you see," explained Mister Yardpole. "Very different to most horses, in this regard — just when your typical chicken gives every indication that she's grasped what you might call the fundamentals of riding a horse, she'll forget everything she ever knew, not excluding the fact that she's a chicken and cannot, as a consequence, fly."

"Easily unhorsed, was she?"

"Like a sack of coals," confirmed Mister Yardpole. "This is why I'm quite satisfied to have had only the one chicken that needed riding lessons — there are numerous and varied other demands on my time, you see." He nodded meaningfully towards the starting gate, where twelve jumpy candidates prepared to compete for the coveted Lawn Bowling Club Open Eight Furlongs bushel of apples, awarded to the first twelve finishers.

"What with Lord Markham's own stables and the boarders, we can have as many as a dozen horses on hand at a time."

"Several hundred, surely, Mister Yardpole."

"Eh?"

"Stilts — Mister Stollery — tells me that, particularly when the National Hunt and Flat seasons overlap, you can have several hundred horses on hand."

"Stilts..." The trainer rested a frayed, cable knit elbow on a darned sleeve and pinched his chin reflectively. "That tall bloke that thinks tall blokes can be jockeys?"

"Sounds like him."

"Well, he's wrong about that, too," said Mister Yardpole. "In fact, when the National Hunt and Flat seasons overlap, we have nearly two hundred horses on hand."

"You don't say."

"Makes me wonder where I find the time to train chickens, never mind horses."

Yardpole raised his binoculars to the starting gate where the inexperienced runners were having difficulty understanding the point, so he instead scanned the crowd.

"Well, what do you make of that?" He lowered his spyglass. "There's half a horse at the tea ladies tent."

Teddy followed his gaze. As promised, six tea ladies now clattered and nattered in the empty tent while the front half of a pantomime horse stood aloof.

"That's not half a horse," differed Teddy.

"Oh, no?"

"Two quarter horses. Hard to tell at this distance." Teddy paused as the Lawn Bowling Eight Furlongs got off to what turned out to be a false start, when a frolicky filly called Shoesby spotted an errant bobbin of candyfloss. "Talking of distance, Mister Yardpole, how did you manage to get such an improved performance out of Chockit Rockit at the Cheveley Handicap?"

Mister Yardpole watched with interest as once again the ribbon was dropped to start the race but only three horses appeared to take the meaning, the others either examined the track for whatever grazing there was to be had or faced the wrong direction. Then he regarded Teddy with an earnest eye and tapped his own temple to emphasise the word, "Training."

"Of course," flattered Teddy. "But have you any views on why Chockit Rockit's results had been so poor in the five races preceding this remarkable victory?"

"Were his results poor?"

"Last place, by all accounts," reported Teddy, "by a considerable distance, measured in furlongs, in fact, and in at least one case quarters of an hour."

Yardpole nodded in studied reflection, as one turning over a thousand factors and sifting as many conditions. Finally, he said, "Chockit Rockit, you say."

"You don't suppose it could be something esoteric, do you Mister Yardpole?" asked Teddy. "The weather or the presence of balloons at the racecourse or, I don't know, Irish reels?"

"Irish reels?"

"As an example."

"No, Miss, not Irish reels." Yardpole shook his head decisively, but was then distracted as, it turned out, the race had got off to a mainly successful, eight-horse start. "No horse is going to go from last place to first for any Irish reel."

"Not even *Dunmore Lasses?*"

"There's only one way you'll see a change that great come over a horse," said Mister Yardpole with his binoculars to his eyes, "and that's cheating."

CHAPTER SIX

For which the reader is provided this useful lexicon: Adam (and Eve) / believe, Brussels (sprout) / doubt, Cambridge University / certainty, Charing (Cross) / hoss / horse, China (plate) / mate, dickie (bird) / word, elephant's trunk / drunk, common (sense) / pence, cunning (spies) / disguise, field (hockey) / jockey, French (braid) / trade, George / pound, give (and get) / bet, half'a (quart) / short, Harvey (Nichols) / pickle / problem, His All Aboard (Ship) / Lordship, Joe Brown / town, moillet / hornless cow / slow horse, never (near) / beer, pram (and stroller) / Roller / Rolls Royce, rainy Sunday / long / length, round (the houses) / trousers, square a tick / settle a debt, twist (and twirl) / girl, ugly step(-sister) / solicitor, Uncle (Ben) / ten, weasel (and stoat) / coat, weighty nun / eighty-to-one.

A LOITERING BUTLER is as close as to an oxymoron as can be had at a village fête, even more so than 'entertaining sack race' and 'desirable tombola prize.' Nevertheless, a loitering butler is precisely what met Teddy as she quit the grounds following the final race of the day, The Middleditch News Agent, Tobacconist, and Conveyancer's Half-Mile for Appaloosas and Palominos Born After Saint Swithins. Despite the dichotomy, Teddy, immediately and without ever seeing him before, instantly recognised, "Marshpool?"

Marshpool was a butlerian sort of butler, trim and slim and pressed into a three-piece morning suit, and complete with factory-issued middle-age, including the optional grey sideburns. In short, even in light of the loitering which, in fact, stretched to leaning against a newel post at the top of the stairs leading down to the castle grounds, he was very clearly Marshpool, the butler.

Nevertheless, he replied, "No."

"No?"

"That is to say, yes, madam."

"Having a bit of a calm repose?" asked Teddy, with the easy empathy she has with domestic servants in general and those who work for her extended relations in particular.

"No, Miss." Marshpool snapped to his full height and gestured to a pair of Wellington boots, stood upside down on the steps. "I was allowing His Lordship's boots to dry before bringing them in."

"And having a quick smoke."

Marshpool raised a prideful chin.

"With respect, madam, I submit that someone has been telling tales about me."

"There's a lit cigarette in your hand."

The butler raised the smoking gun and examined it as though for the first time. Internally, he rapidly reviewed the most immediate declarations and had settled on claiming that he was holding the cigarette for someone when it occurred to him that Teddy was probably clairvoyant, and might as well know all.

"I'm also having a bit of a nip, as defence against the damp." He withdrew a slim flask from his waistcoat. "It's just house brandy, but if madam would care for a snoot..."

"Best save it for your own purposes, Marshpool — I'm family, and can drink openly and to excess."

"Most considerate madam." Marshpool tipped the flask briefly to his lips and then regarded it with a balance of resignation and disappointment. "It was empty anyway. Can I trust that madam will find no call to repeat my indiscretions..."

"Pish, Marshpool, you call those indiscretions? Where were you before Middelditch? Canterbury Cathedral?"

"I was second butler at Handsome Hall, the country seat of Lord Stibling."

"I know the man and the place well," said Teddy. "They ever let you ring the dinner gong?"

"That was my chief occupation."

"Was it now?" asked Teddy. "How long have you been at Middleditch, Marshman?"

"I arrived in the new year, madam." Marshpool suddenly and inefficiently slapped away the remains of the cigarette that was now burning his fingers.

"Replacing Northbridge?"

"I believe so."

"Northbridge operated a fully-functioning speakeasy in the oubliette," recalled Teddy. "A very lively joint it was, too. I was there the night they traded house orchestras with The Blue Lagoon."

"Is this why Mister Northbridge was let go?"

"Just my point, Marshmallow — he wasn't let go, not even after Bobby Howzat was arrested for sedition when he premiered 'I Could Tell You Some Things About the King' in the estate chapel," explained Teddy. "No, Northbridge moved on to a position at Windsor Castle, heading up the commis staff and managing the cabaret."

"I... see..."

"The point is you have nothing to worry about," Teddy assured him. "There are rumours, in fact, that Lord Markham himself has been fiddling the races."

"I can tell you for a certainty that's not so, Miss." Marshpool spoke in hushed and earnest tones and, as a touch of chummy verisimilitude, he lit another cigarette. "What's more, I can tell you the source of those rumours."

"Go on then."

"His Lordship himself." Marshpool scanned the immediate area for spies. "That's all I'm at liberty to say, except that there's nothing to it."

"He thinks he did it with his violin," supplied Teddy, going no distance at all in undermining her reputation for clairvoyance.

"Irish reels," confided Marshpool because, at this point, why not?

"Does the rest of the staff know about this?"

"Just me, Miss." Marshpool drew covetously on his cigarette and then, by force of habit, hid it behind his back. "He often brings me along to the stables to turn the pages of the sheet music."

"Probably best to keep it that way." Teddy made to continue down the stairs. "By the way, Marshmain, do you know where one might find Mister Stollery?"

"Are you Miss Quillfeather, Miss?"

"Are you a police officer?"

"Eh?"

"Yes, I'm Miss Quillfeather."

"Mister Stollery asked me to give you this." Marshpool produced a small envelope and handed it to Teddy, who opened it and read to herself...

'What ho, Tedds — trotted off to a trotter's trough, on the trail of a topping tip. Come to the Martingale pub at your converliest if you want to know how the nobbler nobbled.

Yours forever and ever.

Tilden.'

"Do you know where this pub is, Marshpool?" asked Teddy.

"No, Miss," replied the butler with lightning reflexes. "I mean to say, which pub would that be, madam?

"Don't all butlers read all messages?"

Stilts raised this point of domestic order from a window bench on the wall of the bustling, bubbling Martingale, a pub the location of which Teddy knew well and which, in any case, would have been hard to miss by anyone walking down the town's only high street. The Martingale was one of four pubs in Middleditch on a street crowded with liveries, saddlers, farriers, blacksmiths, feed stores, tack shops, boot cobblers, boot repairers, boot resellers, cartwrights, wainwrights, wheelwrights, and a hair stylist (specialising in manes and tails).

"I expect knowing the household secrets is one of the chief curses of the job," agreed Teddy. "I recall Bamber Rafferty's valet, Chipnall. He knew that Bamber's uncle had cut off his allowance fully a week before Bamber did. Poor chap had to say nothing and wait for the official word from the trustee before he could nick all the silver."

On the table before Stilts and Teddy stood three pints of bitter and behind them was a brightly variegated stained glass window that the grey light of day managed to make monochrome, but the pub interior was the warm palette of the friendly local — golden brass fittings on a rosewood bar, burgundy upholstery beneath amber table tops teetering with tankards of blonde beer, and a glowing orange fire. The theme was picked up, extended, and ultimately exceeded by the clientele, for the Martingale was a pub for punters and those they made rich, and the bookies and touts and jockeys and gamblers relied, in one way or another, on being noticed. Even the air of the crowded pub was garish with garlic butter, pork pie, curry, sausage, and negligently maintained cooking surfaces.

Presently, the *raison d'être* of the third pint of bitter materialised at the door in the form of the brashest, flashest mismatch of colours and cross-patterns in a pub that already looked like the nation's music hall comedians meeting up for a jolly day of golf. He was as tall as a beagle peering over a gate and only then because he was wearing track-side tall-boots, but he was as packed and compact as a barrel of flour and wrapped in a wardrobe that could have lit up a mineshaft. His coat and trousers were of irreconcilable tartans and his waistcoat was the same, except diagonal. He wore a canary cravat through a cardinal collar and his boutonniere was just short of a bouquet. To Teddy's considerable delight, the spectacle spotted Stilts, waved, and ambled over, a journey which occupied two boisterous minutes of the slapping of backs and gripping of hands and whispering of confidences.

"All right, Stilts, me ol' china *(How are you, Stilts, my friend)?*" He pulled off his Union Jack topper and plumped into the proffered captain's chair.

"Teddy Quillfeather, this is Oy Roy, the betting man's better man," presented Stilts. "Oy, this is Teddy, the woman I love."

"You want me to Adam you and this twist, John *(You expect me to believe that this is your sweetheart, Stilts)?*" doubted Oy Roy.

"Didn't say that, Oy." Stilts slid the bookie a pint of bitter. "But I'll keep you informed as matters progress. Do you own a formal suit?"

"Got the weasel for these rounds *(I have the coat that goes with these trousers).*" Oy drew thirstily on his pint and, as he would do more or less constantly, he surveyed the crowd. Two morticians, in terms of comparative dress sense, were sat at the next table, backing and cheering their respective favourite of two raindrops racing for the bottom of the window pane. At the next table along, a game of shove ha'penny had drawn a crowd and a betting pool now in excess of a hundred pounds. At the bar three men who looked more like brothers than do most brothers were borrowing from the landlord the official pub copy of *The Complete Works of William Shakespeare*, to settle whether Claudius or Laertes died first and, hence, who would buy the next round.

"Oy knows all the punters," Stilts assured Teddy. "If anyone can tell us who was made minty by Chockit Rockit's sudden burst of inspiration, it's our old Uncle Oy."

"You know about Chockit Rockit's surprising win at Newmarket, Oy?" asked Teddy.

"I do." Oy nevertheless whet his recollection on a slice of beer. "Six rainy Sundays paying a weighty nun *(Winning by six lengths at odds of eighty-to-one)?* It's the kind of thing that gets noticed, in my line."

"As you might expect if you knew Stanley Lord Bitterbrook, an objection has been raised," continued Teddy. "And as would be equally obvious if you knew my uncle, Markham Lord Middleditch, there's nothing to it. Uncle Markham is the sort of baa lamb that makes other baa lambs go 'aww' while Lord Bitterbrook is widely and justifiably known as 'Sticky' on account of his generous capacity for forgetting a loan, provided it's been made to him."

Oy nodded authoritatively. "The artful *(dodger)* is known to me. And as no one will take his bets on the cuff, no one will take his bets."

"Quite sure?" urged Teddy.

"Without a Brussels. Last time Lord Bitterbrook squared a tick, his ugly step rolled up in a pram to offer me an Uncle common on a George *(Without a doubt. Last time I collected on a debt from Lord Bitterbrook, his solicitor came round in a Rolls Royce to offer ten pence to the pound)."*

"He means yes," clarified Stilts. "Lord Bitterbrook is barred from betting, certainly with any bookie that could handle a wager worth cheating to win."

"Well, that's disappointing — I was very much hoping that we were going to get irrefutable evidence that Lord Bitterbrook was somehow behind the crime." Teddy drew meditatively on her pint. "I suppose we'll just have to fit him up for it, instead."

"I don't say His All Aboard *(His Lordship)* never lays a bet," cautioned Oy. "There's no preventing one geezer from backing a horse on behalf of another. Sir Ludlow Royce-Phipps, as an example, used to place all his bets through his chauffeur. Poor business, from my point of view, all that sort of thing, because Sir Ludlow never could pick a winner, and his chauffeur retired to private life on what he saved playing the odds — he only actually placed one wager out of five."

"Then we're back where we were." Teddy paused for a moment of uproar as the coin dropped off the shove ha'penny field of play and twelve bets were placed on heads or tails before it hit the floor. "So, since we can't know who profited from Chockit Rockit's win, we'll have to work out how it was done. I don't suppose you know how it was done, do you, Oy?"

"With a solid Cambridge *(certainty)."*

"Not really."

"There's only one way to manage a horse of the calibre of Chockit Rockit to that extent over that many fixtures." Oy drew a dramatic draw of bitter. "The field bottled him *(the jockey held him back)*"

"Well, you'll be happy to know that your view is shared by no less informed company than the Middleditch village fête tea ladies," said Teddy. "And they represent a powerful voting block. Can you prove it?"

Oy glanced from side to side, then discreetly withdrew his pocket triangle — or at any rate, he withdrew it as discreetly as one can a pocket triangle formed of a burst of lime-green chiffon — and gave it a little wave over his shoulder.

Two miniature men, whom Teddy hadn't noticed beneath the surface of the crowd, and who'd been standing on the brass rail at the bar such that they might reach their pints, conferred briefly and then navigated the sea of hips and elbows between the bar and Teddy's table. They liberated two adjacent stools and climbed up to table level.

The men were jockeys, if it needs be said, known as Flat Milliken and Pudge Hillock. Flat was called Flat ironically and seasonally — during the National Hunt season he would claim that he was best on the flats, and vice-versa, and so during the Flat season he was known as Jump Milliken. It was, at the time, the beginning of Flat season but, for the sake of clarity, Jump is herein referred to as Flat. Like many jockeys Flat was a serious-minded professional with an almost monastic dedication to the spiritual and material demands of his sport, except on days when he isn't riding, when things tend to balance out with perhaps a bit of a handicap favouring the need of any hard-working athlete to relax with a dozen anonymous acquaintances and a cask of Midlands brandy.

Pudge was also ironically nicknamed by his peers. He was even shorter than the average jockey, a physical asset that Pudge employed to advantage during training, typically in the form of two pints of Guinness with a lunch of sausage and chips while Flat, a full two-inches taller, could only look on in quiet agony.

In contradistinction to Flat, who, like Charlemagne and record-holding three-year-old Derby winner Call Boy, owes none of his success to formal education, Pudge went to Cambridge, and his family owns several of the horses he's ridden to his most notable victories.

Both men were extravagantly conspicuous, in that they were dressed in quiet browns and rust tweeds, plump woollen scarves, and cloth caps pulled low and, in the case of Flat, turned backwards.

Introductions were made and Teddy asked the obvious, "Should jockeys be openly socialising in a tout trade pub?"

"Most absolutely not," said Pudge. "Our calling is quite alive to the standing of that to which it refers, euphemistically, if you're asking me, as 'appearances'."

"Which is why we don't never come here," explained Flat.

"Never," agreed Pudge, and the two men tapped together their tankards and drank deeply. "Who's round is it?"

"Mine!" Stilts very nearly shouted for, to his mind, he was in the company of greatness. Here were men who had achieved not only normal height but, from his perspective, they had defeated it, and built on that remarkable victory a career in the only field that could be fairly called poetry, or divine.

Pudge quickly took Stilts' measure. "Whisky, I think."

"You don't need to be making two trips to the bar," sympathised Flat, "if you make 'em large ones."

Stilts danced off to the bar and Teddy continued the subversive small talk.

"So, how do you come to know Oy Roy?"

"We don't," replied Flat.

"Never met the man," added Pudge. "And we don't care to. Doubtless he's a lovely chap, but it would never do to be seen associating with a bookmaker."

' He's a bookie, is he?" Flat asked his colleague.

' So I'm led to understand." Pudge finished his pint. "One hears rumours."

Oy Roy nodded in sober accord. "My French *(trade)* is every bit as tetchy — I must be ever mindful to never be seen in the company of a jockey. Sad, I call it, how quick the corrupted mind is to see conspiracy where there's just a matey never *(beer)*. Do you recall the unfortunate circumstances of poor Eachway Archie?"

"No," confirmed Pudge and Flat, and they both nodded gravely.

"Warned off for life," added Flat.

"And all for the love of finer things," continued Pudge. "Poor Archie was, in addition to one of Southern England's most cutthroat handicappers, an aficionado of architecture. During the week, if there wasn't a race, he would unfailingly be profiting from the practice introduced of late by many aesthetically rich but economically impoverished estates — a day of opening to the public."

"Unlucky is the only word for it," judged Oy, "that he happened to elect to visit the same houses on the same days as Nefyn Lord Knebbly."

"Who had, at the time, a promising stable of hurdlers," filled in Flat.

"All down to appearances," lamented Pudge. "It was concluded by the stewards that Eachway Archie and Lord Knebbly were meeting not in their capacity as connoisseurs of baileys and barbicans, but to exchange inside information that Archie would exploit on the lively tips market."

"He was though, wasn't he?" supposed Teddy.

"Well, of course he was," said Oy.

"But it were appearances what sunk him," lamented Flat. "I happen to know, though, personally and for sure, that Archie was planning to retire that same year."

"Bought Spill Hill Hall, in Sussex," added Pudge.

"Rechristened it Eachway 'All," concluded Flat.

"Open to the public, as perhaps a deliberate point of irony, every first and third Sunday," epiologued Pudge.

"Appearances." Oy reintroduced the theme. "This is why these two men, who are strangers to me, can never come to this pub."

In that moment Stilts stumbled out of the crowd, expertly encircling five drinks within two hands.

"Sorry for the delay — three chaps were wagering on my exact height and they wouldn't take my word for it, so a measure had to be found."

"Pudge and Flat, who aren't here and never have been, are absolutely not about to tell us who the jockey was who held back Chockit Rockit," recounted Teddy.

"No, we aren't," protested Pudge as he received his large whisky from Stilts.

"No, I know that," agreed Teddy. "You're not even here."

"He means that no jockey never nobbled Chockit Rockit," clarified, he thought, Flat.

"How can you be so sure?" asked Teddy.

"Because I was Chockit Rockit's jockey." Flat toasted his quick retort and drank deeply. "Except when I weren't."

"When weren't you?"

"For a brief period from early March to only last week." Flat finished his whisky by a length. "I was indisposed."

In fact, for six weeks Flat was unable or, to be legalistically accurate, unwilling to leave home, for he had cause to believe that the police were looking for him. He had no recollection of why the police might be looking for him but he had, nevertheless, solid grounds — he awoke on a Sunday morning with a black eye and a manacle on one wrist. Experience had shown Flat that the best course of action when this or something astonishingly similar happens is to sit tight.

"Well then that, obviously, is when Chockit Rockit was nobbled," pointed out Teddy. "Who was your replacement?"

"Pudge."

"Oh."

Pudge finished his drink and slid the empty glass suggestively towards Stilts. "And I did not hold back Chockit Rockit. The horse simply didn't have the legs for it. To me the mystery isn't how he lost five races in a row, but how it is he ever won anything."

"Who's round is it, now?" Flat wanted to know.

"Mine!" enthused Stilts.

"Can you manage?" wondered Pudge, adding as an aside to

Flat. "It strikes me our friend struggled rather with two whiskies and three pints last round, poor chap."

"I have an idea," said Flat, thinking quickly but deeply, "what if we was to lend a hand."

"I say, capital idea, Flat," congratulated Pudge. "We could save our friend as many as two more trips to the bar."

The happy hunting party departed in boisterous spirits, looking like two kindly gnomes escorting a telegraph pole across a busy street.

"Can they be trusted?" Teddy asked Oy.

"Who?" Oy replied, rather in line with expectations, now Teddy thought about it.

"Speaking in the abstract, Oy, do jockeys ever nobble horses on which they've bet?"

"Never." Oy waved away the notion like a noxious odour. "Jockeys never bet on horses they ride."

"Oh, do come along, Oy," protested Teddy. "Or do you mean to say they never bet on horses they ride in the same manner in which they never come into this pub?"

"I don't know if you'll have tumbled a physical peculiarity shared by the two gentlemen who weren't here just now," commented Oy.

"They're short."

"They are," agreed Oy. "And 'ow's a mucker like that going to make 'is daily if not flying the four-footer, if he was ever to be warned off? No, Teddy, it's past perilous for a field to lay a give on his own Charing."

"I'm authoritatively informed that one geezer can easily lay a bet on behalf of another geezer," Teddy reminded him.

"I congratulate you, Teddy, on your tight and trustworthies, but few fields in the field have that luxury." Oy toasted Teddy's steady circle of friends.

"A disguise, then?" suggested Teddy. "I have an aunt who does a very convincing pantomime horse — convincing might not be quite the right word, let us say committed — and I myself only recently stood in for Tilly Fivequidder before one of His Majesty's magistrates who are, as a breed, suspicious."

Cy nodded towards Flat, who was boosting Pudge up so that he could order from the landlord, "There's no cunning for a bloke so half'a that wouldn't make him even more conspicuous."

"No, I see your point." Teddy imbibed a bitter bit of bitter. "But none of that holds for the average punter, so we've no way of knowing who it was who placed the winning bet on Chockit Rockit."

"I don't say that, Teddy." Oy assumed as serious a countenance as can be expected of a man wearing three different plaids. "I can make the speech, and I will, all provided I'm in a position to do so, but I'm in the froth meself, and every inch as deep as Lord Markham and the greater Joe."

"Okay..." Teddy considered this announcement carefully before saying, "What?"

"I'm in as much trouble as Lord Markham, Teddy," translated Oy, "and if you can't help me we're both ruined, along with the entire town of Middleditch."

CHAPTER SEVEN

Featuring surprising sources of unwelcome revelations and spuds.

"HOW CAN A BOOKIE BE RUINED, Oy?" Teddy wanted to know "You literally own the casino."

"Me hedges."

"I don't know that one," confessed Teddy. "Hedges and hurdles? Girdles? Is it your girdle that's troubling you?"

"My literal and lateral hedges, Teddy," muddied Oy. "Hedge bets. All bookies lay off their bets, especially the longers and lessers, when they get a bit too top-heavy. When I carry that much risk, I place counter-bets with other bookies, sharing out the damage should a long-odds moillet take the gate. Of late, I've had cause to spread my hedges well past comfort, which is bad enough, but then as often as not, that same surprise nag will be disqualified."

"Why are you placing more hedge bets than usual?"

"That's me second Harvey — someone is tipping off me regulars to random longshots who then go on to win." Oy looked into his beer as into a foggy, faulty crystal ball. "It's put me right off me game, it has, and an odds-maker can be a right elephant's, he can, or he can be flat barmy, but there's no firm long term for a book what's off his game."

"Well, that's certainly clear enough." Teddy cast an eye towards Stilts, who was buying rounds for an uncountable number of admirers, and the jockeys, who were sitting on the bar. "Current demands on my services are many and varied, Oy, but just as soon as I've sorted out this fiddling business with Uncle Markham I'd be happy to lend you my expertise in picking clinkers. Doubtless you know that I selected every single winner but one of the classics last year."

"You picked four winners out of five fixtures?"

"Very nearly. In all five races I picked the winner but for one horse — the actual winner."

"It's a conspiracy, Teddy." Oy surveyed once again the gambolling, gambling gaggle and then shifted his stool closer to the table. "I need someone outside the game, someone I can trust, to sort it before I'm for it."

"What makes you think I'm the one to sort it, Oy?"

"Stilts tells me it's in your line." Oy glanced at the bar where the Stilts in question was once again being measured, this time in jockeys. "And I don't know no one else outside the game."

"I'm flattered. And so while I'm uncovering and putting an end to an industry-wide conspiracy, you'll be finding out who bet large on Chockit Rockit for the Cheveley Handicap, are those the rough terms of the arrangement?"

"Upon my Richard."

❦

"Richard the Third — word."

Stilts explained the obvious from the pointless end of the reins of the two-wheeled sulky drawn through the foggy, cloggy evening by the indifferent coach horse.

"What have you signed me — I beg your pardon, slight correction — what have you signed us up for, Stilts?" Teddy enquired from the comparative comfort and cover of a burlap horse blanket.

"A jest of a quest, if nothing else." Stilts leaned into the darkness and, seeing nothing, urged the horse on. "It will bring us closer together."

"Or make of us mortal enemies," observed Teddy. "You've always been such a sportsman, Stilts."

"Oy's an exceptionally sound apple, Tedds, even for a bookie," said Stilts as he tried and failed to control an entertaining oversteer.

"Loves his granny, does he?"

"I should hope so — she's one of his best leg men." In reply to an overcorrection to the oversteer, Stilts leaned onto Teddy. "Sorry. Slippy road."

Teddy peered over the edge to evaluate said slippiness. "Are the wheels even turning?"

"Well, of course the wheels are turning… ha! No. Brake's on."
Stilts adjusted accordingly to no discernable difference in ride nor
velocity.

'Do you trust that Oy Roy will help us identify who bet big
on Chockit Rockit if we help him sort out his long shot losses?"

"Why, Teddy, of course he will," protested Stilts. "The man's a
bookie, and he gave you his Richard." He added a calming "There
there" directed towards the horse who was, in fact, half asleep.
"And whether he can help us or not, Tedds, we have to work out
how the list of long odds leaders are being disqualified. It's
ruining Oy, the poor turnip."

"Is it, Stilts?" wondered Teddy. "He reminded me a bit of Crib
Digby."

'In that they're both slaves to fashion?"

'There's that," allowed Teddy, "but I was referring more to
last New Year's, when Crib had a bit of a hangover, he paid off his
debts and engaged Robert Bridges to write his eulogy."

"Who knew there were so many synonyms for 'despair'."

"You don't think that Oy likes to season his stories with a
souçon of slant?" asked Teddy. "He told me that if we can't stop
all these disqualifications, not only will he have to slide the key
under the door, so will the whole of Middleditch."

"Oh, right…" Stilts slackened the reins, such that the horse
might ease up his pace on the straight. "He told you about the
farm then, did he?"

"Of course."

"Well, that's all right then."

"Okay, no, Oy didn't tell me about any farm. What farm?"

"It's a secret."

"Yes, I gathered that, Stilts, now tell it to me."

"Right oh — Oy keeps a farm for retired racehorses." Now at a
fork in the road, Stilts guided the horse to the left. The horse went
right, because that was the way home.

"Why does Oy Roy keep a farm for retired racehorses?"

"Because if he didn't they'd meet a very sticky end indeed. Do
you know how glue is made, Tedds?" The carriage slid slowly to a
near stop. Stilts flicked the reins encouragingly and, to clarify the
point, said, "Hup hup hup," before realising that the horse had
slowed up behind a Clydesdale towing a Bentley Three.

"Then why is it a secret?"

"Oy's a bookie, Tedds," Stilts reminded her. "He can't have the punters knowing he has anything like a heart. The greater ground, though, is that the farm itself has to remain a secret as a matter of economy — the horses are bought by the pound for parts, you understand. If the truth were to become known then the asking price would be for that of a live, fully-functioning horse, probably sold at auction."

"What goes on at a farm for retired racehorses, when it comes to that?"

"A tremendous amount of frolicking, romping, capering — what you might call horseplay, now I think of it — and quite a bit of sweeping in formation across the vales and meadows." Stilts, briefly forgetting the reins, leaned out and looked back down the road, on which they were now being followed by a Morris-Cowley touring edition, towed by a donkey. "The farm is an immense stretch of Middleditch..." Stilts nodded at the fog curtain rising from the ditch on the left side of the road. "We've been passing it for about fifteen minutes now."

"The farm is here in Middleditch?" marvelled Teddy. "It's a well-kept secret indeed."

"It's disguised as a riding school. Rather clever cover, when you want to hide horses in plain sight, don't you think?"

"Why not actually make it a riding school?"

"Lolly, mainly." Stilts nodded at the still-passing retirement farm. "At these initial stages, Oy has focused on rescuing the ageing trotter. Kitting out a riding school is what he calls phase two."

"How long has phase one been going on?"

"Ten years..." Stilts spoke with an awed realisation. "Fifteen if you count — actually it's been fifteen. And all that time Oy's been keeping it going with what, until quite recently, has been a very rich vein of bookmaking."

"And the town has grown increasingly reliant on providing equestrian services to the phoney pony school," concluded Teddy.

"Roughly half the economy of Middleditch is Oy Roy's refuge for the tired, retired and unrequired," agreed Stilts. "The other half, of course, is dependent upon Lord Markham's stables, unless and until it's warned off."

"Well, this is all falling together very nicely, Stilts." Teddy put her feet up on the dash rail, as one does in a carriage going walking speed. "All we have to do is work out how and why so many long shots are being disqualified starting, I think it stands to reason, with whoever it is who's tipping off Oy's customers with seemingly random heifers who somehow go on to win. Should be a walkover."

"You really think so, Tedds?"

"No, Stilts, I do not," levied Teddy. "I was being ironic. We also have to work out who nobbled Chockit Rockit and how, but I suppose for the moment we can leave it with Oy Roy to find out who placed the single big bet on the Cheveley Handicap."

The carriage slanted as it slid slightly ditchwards, causing Stilts to recall that he was meant to be driving. He took up the reins but, it turned out, the horse had been making allowance for an Austin 7 coming the other way, towed by a tractor which was, in turn, towed by two Shires.

"Sloppy night," observed Stilts. "How do we proceed, Tedds?"

"The winning long shots, I think," assessed Teddy. "As Oy tells it, he's significantly increased his hedge betting — the long-odds wagers he lays off with other bookies — because someone is giving his regulars reliable tips on long shots. Stranger still, the punters who'll own up to it tell Oy that the tout who's selling them the tips is a sweet, silver-haired old lady."

"That's not his granny," Stilts assured her. "She dyes her hair a colour she calls 'sorrel'. What does Oy's old lady look like?"

"Apart from sweet, little, old, and grey-haired, you mean?"

"I do."

"He doesn't know," said Teddy. "In fact, he only knows she exists because so many punters are telling him that they got their winning tip from her."

"Why doesn't she bet them herself, if she's so dab?"

"I don't know — why does any tout not bet?"

"They do, though," countered Stilts, "if they know they've got a winner."

"Really?" Teddy squinted into the darkness until sure that it held no answers. "This sounds like it might prove relevant, in time, along with another strange aspect of the affair — as often as not — oftener, from Oy's perspective — the winning long shot hedge bet is subsequently disqualified for any number of reasons, indicating either an epidemic of cheating or an unprecedented increase in vigilance — the latter being the more likely, because no two disqualifications are ever the same. Typically, in fact, it's not even cheating, in the traditional sense — wrong owner name in the registration or no owner name or the wrong horse name, or the horse, at the end of the race, is somehow carrying less weight than that which he was handicapped at the start."

Teddy spoke here of one of the many competing usages of the word 'handicapping' in the sport of kings, in this case it refers to the practice of adding weight — typically in the form of lead bars — to a horse's saddle with a view to evening out the race. The objective is to create a more sporting event with an unguessable result with which, if anyone at all is happy, it's a matter of pure luck.

The weights are typically (but, as will soon become significant, not always) ascribed by track stewards, and enforced by the simple precaution of 'weighing in' a jockey and his gear before the race, followed by a 'weighing out' directly after.

"Sounds more slipshod than slick fraud," said Stilts. "If a horse is meant to be carrying a total ten stone, as an example, and he's not, as a further example, it'll be found out. Same for a botched card — if the horse wins, the registration becomes the official record."

With a start, Stilts realised once again that he'd been neglecting the reins. He took them up and listed like a tethered mast, calling out an urgent "Whoa!"

"Oh." Stilts smiled happy surmise at Teddy. "We'd already stopped." He squinted into the misty night. "Where are we?"

In that instant a brass-bright gas light whelmed over them as Marshpool opened the front door of Middleditch Castle.

"A messenger awaits without, Miss, at the service entrance."

Innocuous as this message might appear, Marshpool shared it with Teddy as a discreet aside, very nearly incoherently out of the corner of his mouth, while tipping a stipple of after-dinner tipple into her glass. At the time, the ladies had retired to the games room, leaving Stilts with the various lordships to choke on cigars and affect a knowledge of brandy.

Teddy excused herself, claiming that she felt under-dressed in present company — Lady Bitterbrook was in a simple teal silk beaded gold-embroidered evening dress from Callot Soeurs that would feature, to much comment, later that summer in a special edition of *Vogue* magazine dedicated to that dress and the marcelled bob, and Lady Markham was, consequently, in a smoke-grey satin Callot Soeurs formal that she had planned on first wearing at Ascot. Lady Bitterbrook regarded Teddy sympathetically over her sherry and said, "Of course, dear. Do your best," and wished her luck.

In the warm and sultry castle kitchen, sat at the cutting table by the fire, was Chard, the leg man. He was wearing a red blazer that he won off a Sullihill day boy in a strong lay against the sentimental favourite in the Sullihill-Picklescott cricket match, and he was warming his hands over a steaming cup of tea.

"Evening Miss."

"What ho, Chard." Teddy assumed the perpendicular corner and a zone of confidentiality, as the cook busied herself at the preserves counter. "I understand you have a message for me?"

"Oh, no Miss. I think there must have been a misunderstanding between myself and that nice Mister Marshpool," claimed Chard. "It was someone else I come to see, on business I'm not at liberty to divulge."

"Spoke to Oy Roy, did you?"

"I don't know that I'm able to say that the name is familiar to me, Miss."

"Stubby former jockey who favours a cross-hatched clash of colour you could hear from Cornwall?" described Teddy helpfully. "Speaks in Cockney rhyming slang, a vast racecourse lexicon, and a patois of his own invention?"

'You might be surprised at how many gentlemen of my acquaintance would answer to that very description, Miss."

'Would it narrow the suspects a bit if I were to mention that Oy Roy has agreed to help me identify the party who bet large on Chockit Rockit's surprising victory at Newmarket?"

"Might do," admitted Chard. "There is a bloke I've heard of, could be the bloke in question, who has of late been spreading his hedges thin as spilled beer, and is betting his little all on a fast-talking stiletta up from London."

"You should introduce us. Sounds like we'd have loads in common."

"Wouldn't mind having a moment with the lady myself. If I did, I'd likely take the opportunity to describe the stakes as, at the risk of appearing to exaggerate, whacking."

"She knows, Chard."

"I was referring to me livelihood, to give it a name, and that of me mum."

"The one with the recipes."

"That's the mum I mean, yes, the one with the recipes."

"She's not a sweet little old lady who sells tips at the track, is she?"

"Me mum is thirty-seven, and she's barmaid at the Cricketers, where she sometimes does a high-kicking routine, unbid. The lady what's been passing winners to Oy Roy's clients appears to be a full-time tout, and in fact has made a legend and a nuisance of herself, in equal measure, from Middleditch to Bromford Bridge." Chard added, "Oh, thank you, ma'am," to the cook who, smiling indulgently, set a roast beef sandwich on the table before him.

"They know you here, do they?"

"Not as such, no Miss." Chard took a bite that was a testament to the quality of the roast beef sandwich made at Middleditch Castle. "I told the cook I was your brother. She didn't believe it, of course, even for an instant, but she called me a scamp, tossled me hair, and give me a cup of tea."

"Any idea how the little old lady is picking consistent winners?"

Chard put down his sandwich and regarded it as though just then realising what a marvel sandwiches are. "You'll never credit it, Miss, but it never occurred to me to ask myself that." He regarded Teddy with a master class of flat sarcasm. "Fancy that. I could probably have made myself a neat little retirement trousseau by now had I thought to work out how it is this little old lady knows which long shots are going to win."

'Assuming they're not disqualified," pointed out Teddy.

'Assuming, as you say, Miss, they're not disqualified." Chard took up his sandwich. "Which is the second and notably knottier bit of gristle in the pie — Oy Roy's losing his knack for laying off the risk, now he sees risk in every little old lady, and so many of his hedge bets are managing to bodge the job by a technicality that the poor bloke's losing the very joy of the game, not to mention substantial profits."

'And you've no notion what's causing those disqualifications, either, I take it," took Teddy.

Chard shook his head as a placeholder activity while he chewed and swallowed. "Not the slightest slant. It's never deliberate, to the unsuspecting eye or even the suspecting I. Wrong name, wrong owner, wrong weight, wrong conditions — wrong horse, on at least two occasions."

'Wrong horse? How could that possibly happen?" wondered Teddy. "It's not as though they're interchangeable, like other people's brollies or taxis or box seats at the Criterion."

'One instance was two bay horses with no special markings, and another was two chestnuts what describe similar, and only the one stable lad both times," explained Chard. "It don't happen when a horse is a limited edition — like Chockit Rockit, who can present different colours depending the position of the sun and direction of the wind — but mistakes will happen with your less exotically stamped plugs."

'Well, that's muddied the waters nicely, thank you, Chard."

'I know it has. Muddy facts will often have that effect, I've found in my time." Chard finished his sandwich and handed his plate, along with a wide, innocent smile, to the cook, and then leaned back into the zone of confidence. "If I was a leg man, which I ain't saying I am, I'd be in a very cutthroat business, Miss. Most heartless it can be, at times. It would be encouraging to a young lad like meself to think that once Mister Roy had done a good turn that it would be returned in kind."

'Good turns are what I do, Chard," Teddy assured him. "I'll have you know that just last month I recovered and returned a valuable penguin stolen from the London Zoo."

'How did you manage that?"

'How did I recover it, you mean?" asked Teddy. "Or how did I nick it in the first place?"

"As you might have learned from parties familiar with the practice, hedge betting is how odds-makers spread their risk — it's like insurance." Chard gave a smile and a wave to the cook, who remained a safe distance, occupied with the oven. "These hedge bets are placed with other bookies, so if there's a sudden increase in disqualified long shots, it affects everyone, if you take my meaning, Miss."

"Not even a little bit, Chard, but I'm growing inured to the sensation."

"It would be helpful for an outsider, such as yourself, to talk to the biggest bookie in the game — the bigger the bookie, the more of his hedges are going south, and the broader his knowledge." Chard once again checked on the cook's distant disinterest. "And the biggest in the business is Jimmy Fairly."

Finally the cook returned, topped up Chard's cup, and gave him a sticky bun and a pat on the head.

"May I offer you anything, Miss?" asked Chard. "I can recommend the sandwiches very highly."

"I'm all right — I've got a glass of sherry and a pot of pomposity waiting for me in the games room. I will have that message you have for me, though."

Chard shook his head earnestly. "As I say, Miss, I come here on business with someone else at the castle." As he spoke, though, Chard reached into the inside pocket of his Ulster, which hung over an adjacent chair and which he won off the father of a Bun Hill boy in a wager on a very tightly contested game of Red Rover. "However, as you're here, perhaps you wouldn't mind relaying this to Her Ladyship — it's just a recipe of me mum's in which she expressed some interest, Third Race Roast Spuds. With ten pounds of potatoes it serves 14-to-1. It's a very popular dish, Miss — I recommend you try it yourself, before the servings shorten to 12 or even ten to one."

"Where's Her Ladyship?"

Teddy asked this of Lady Llewella as a key element of her dramatic return to the games room.

"I'm Her Ladyship."

"The other one," specified Teddy. "The crooked one who bets on long-odds horses that her husband has somehow nobbled for five prior races."

"Lady Bitterbrook."

"If that is her real name."

"She left." Llewella regarded the door. "She didn't say why nor where. She didn't say anything. I think she forgot I was here."

"No matter, Lady Lulu," announced Teddy. "I have here proof that it was Lord Bitterbrook who bet on Chockit Rockit to win the Cheveley Handicap. Now the stewards inquiry will have to find that Uncle Markham couldn't have fiddled the race or, at any rate, wouldn't have, because he couldn't possibly have profited from doing so."

"What proof?"

Teddy produced the recipe for Third Race Roast Spuds and read it aloud, and then held up the paper like she'd once seen a triumphant crown council hold up the driver's licence she'd left in a blind tiger in Soho. "Lady Bitterbrook claimed that she'd never met Richard Purdy — this betting slip proves that to be a pie-faced porky, and in any case the clear, unspoken message from Chard is that the person who placed this bet is the same person who bet on Chockit Rockit."

"Oh. Dear."

There are few ways to say 'Oh. Dear,' that don't sound ominous, reducing to zero when it's accompanied by a frank examination of one's shoes.

"Oh dear?" checked Teddy, still holding the recipe aloft. "Oh. Dear. You're The Ladyship to which Chard referred, aren't you?"

Lady Llewella smiled a sweetly incompetent innocence over her sherry. "Is that a problem, dear?"

"It doesn't help a great deal." Teddy poured herself a therapeutic dose of sherry. "And certainly not as much as would evidence of a Bitterbrook conspiracy, but it may not do much harm if you can convincingly swear that Lord Markham knew nothing about the bet."

"Oh. Dear."

"You told him," guessed Teddy.

"No, I didn't tell him. He told me. He asked me to place the bet on Chockit Rockit to win the Cheveley Handicap."

CHAPTER EIGHT

*In which is examined the complex interplay of bookie and punter,
trainer and charge, chicken and horse.*

SPOONS WAS IN THE MOMENT. Spoons was always in the
moment, of course, but this moment was unique because it was,
in a paradoxically descriptive tautology, unique. Spoons had never
experienced a moment like this one before.

He was at the post, behind the ribbon, and he was one of
eight squirrely two-year-olds scraping and stamping at the grit
waiting for something none of them remembered or understood,
precisely, but which for all of them was the only thing that
mattered. This was all perfectly in line with vague, foggy
expectations, but Spoons wasn't fidgeting and dancing like his
best and only mates in the whole world. He was certainly tense
and ready to do that thing — whatever it was that he was expected
to do — the moment the ribbon fell. He was sure it would come to
him but Spoons felt as sure as he was ever sure of anything that
compared to the last time — the only time that he recalled, ever —
something was missing.

Now the ribbon fell and all the horses shot onto the course as
though fired from cannons and the crisp, brisk morning air was
whistling through his ears, and all around the ground pounded
with the sound of bounding hoofs. Spoons was among his kind,
among the right sort, similar thinkers who all shared exacting and
exactly the same view on the value and vitality of sweeping in a
thundering wave across the savage tundra. The boom and rhythm
kept pace with his heart and he was one part of a roaring, soaring
concord, making his contribution here on the edges, at the back,
out of the way.

Still, something wasn't as it should be. There was a
bright-eyed black stallion leading the herd, but that was probably
all right. Somebody had to do it. The chap on his back with the
sing-songy voice might have been less jolly than in the past, but if

he was honest Spoons never quite understood how that chap fit into things. The shouty spectators were every bit as shouty as ever, and that was nice.

In an instant the moment narrowed on the one difference that mattered — just ahead, near the finishing post, under the arm of Wooly Man, was Chicken, and she was clearly bored and distracted. What seemed years of painful memories came flooding back to Spoons as he rumbled along, trailing the herd — Chicken had ridden out to the parade ground on his head, but she had to be encouraged to do so and even... even bribed. Chicken wouldn't sit on Spoons' head until Woolly Man put some corn in his ears.

Spoons finished a distant last.

"Well, that was a catastrophe."

Teddy made this obvious observation to Mister Yardpole as they waited for the runners to return to the paddock. The trainer had a chicken under his arm and Teddy was tearing up her recipe for First Race Risolles and sighing steam into the mist of the chill morning where it joined the haze of horse, huff, and hide.

The crowd clapped and cheered each entry and a boisterous bonhomie prevailed, but for Spoons, who entered the paddock looking very decidedly last-placey.

"It's the chicken." Yardpole leaned towards Teddy and covered the chicken's ears. "She and Spoons have had words."

"What could a horse and a chicken possibly find to argue about?" wondered, as would anyone, Teddy.

"Sunrise?"

"I could see that." Teddy lowered her voice. "Don't tell me Spoons is one of those swivel-eyed hatters who supports setting the clocks ahead or back or whatever it is we do every spring."

"Back in, oh, let me think — oh-one, I think it was..." Yardpole looked to the chicken for guidance, "...no, that's right — it was last September. We had us a three-year-old stallion hurdler boarding in the stables, name of Whispered Warranty or Pickled Onion or Snick or something very like that. He was staying here while I tried to cure him of his habit of refusing any jump over knee height."

"Who's the chicken in this story?" asked Teddy. "The horse?"

"Nope. He were just plain lazy. Didn't like to be up and doing before ten o'clock, which brings us to the chicken..." Spoons, now unsaddled, was brought to Mister Yardpole, who put the chicken on the horse's head, "...down the road not a mile is an egg and poultry farm, and they had a rooster name of Garibaldi. Like many of his kind and kin, Garibaldi makes it a practice to announce sunrise and he has a voice that do carry, that bird."

"Snick didn't care for it, though," guessed Teddy.

"He did not." Yardpole caught the chicken as she tried to fly away and instead fell like a sack of clumsy rocks. "Cured his jumping problem, though — third morning here, Garibaldi was up with the sun and in specially fine voice, Snick hurdled his stall door, two stable lads, the main gate, a tractor, and a hay wagon, just to get down the road to the egg and poultry farm. No telling what might have happened were Garibaldi not on the roof of the barn — Snick made a good try at it, too, and it were a two-story barn."

"What did happen?"

"Snick's owner give me a hundred quid *poor-bwahr* and bought Garibaldi." Yardpole carefully sprinkled barley seed onto Spoons' mane. "Same season, Snick won Cheltenham Christmas and Kempton Championship, came second in The Victoria Cup, and kicked a Crossley delivery van into a ditch, on account of a horn which sounds quite like a rooster."

There's no way to sugar-coat it — Spoons resented the barley in his hair and he resented why it was there. Within seconds, he'd forgotten there was barley in his hair but the bitter sentiment remained as he trotted back to the stables, an indifferent chicken on his head.

"You want me to talk to them?" offered Teddy. "I have the knack. Stel Digby and Heddy Halibins, to take an example to hand, are fellow members of the Ladies' Auto Club and lifelong friends until they had a falling out. I healed the rift in a single gesture — I claimed it was me, and not Stella, who had modified Heddy's roadmaps just prior to the Norwich to Scunthorpe Rally, making it appear as though Skegness beach was a shortcut."

"That was proper noble of you, Miss."

"She'd have found out eventually."

The wise old trainer shook his head with firm fatalism as he watched Spoons brood into the stable.

"It would be no use, I'm afraid, Miss. If I've seen it once I've seen it a thousand times — it's got to run its course."

"How long does it normally take a chicken and a horse to work out their differences?"

"No saying, with any certainty." Yardpole returned the remaining barley to the barley pocket of his trousers. "Not really an exact science, you understand, but it should be sorted by Monday."

"That sounds pretty exact to me."

"I don't say it will be," clarified Mister Yardpole, "only that it should be — Spoons runs his first sanctioned race on Monday."

"It's quite grave, is it, for a horse to lose his first race? I mean to say, it must happen all the time. Will the other horses tease him? Would you tease him, Mister Yardpole? Is that the secret of your success?"

Teddy and the trainer stepped back to allow a new field of entrants to parade into the paddock in anticipation of the Middleditch Planing Mill Pine Plate for Fillies With Few Prospects.

'Spoons' first sanctioned race is a claim race," explained Yardpole. "It means I have to choose the handicap weight myself, and if his form don't improve before Monday I'll have to make him as light as possible."

'You get to choose the handicap weight?" Teddy eyed her entry, as described in Chard's mum's recipe for Second Event Syllabub. "I thought course management decided how much weight a horse has to carry in handicap races."

'That's so, but for claim races. In a claim race, the handicap is the same for all horses, but I can claim as much as a ten pound reduction."

"Oh, right," Teddy presumed, incorrectly, to have twigged. "You should do that, then. Why doesn't everyone?"

"Because the price is reduced two hundred pounds for every pound of lead that I claim."

"What price?" asked Teddy. "The purse, you mean?"

"No, the price." Yardpole nodded once again his fatalistic nod. "In a claim race, the horses that don't win are sold at the end of the race, for a fixed price less the claim."

"Not really," ghast Teddy. "You don't mean to say that unless he wins on Monday…"

"Yes, Miss — we'll lose Spoons."

On a grassy rise overlooking the crowded fête and the first bend, a correct and clipped valet named Somersby opened a gateleg table onto a Persian rug. He then unfolded a card chair, dusted it with a chamois which he used only for dusting that particular chair, and then spread and perfectly balanced a lace tablecloth, using a tailor's measure. This was followed by a crystal vase for which Somersby opened a mother-of-pearl gun case to select, from a range of five colour options, a single white rose. He laid out the fish knife and escargot fork and consommé spoon and olive skewer and caper pick and specific course silverware, chablis and burgundy glasses, and a napkin in a silver ring.

This concluded, Somersby returned to the silver Rolls Royce Phantom — with coach by Thrupp & Maberly and drawn today by a shiny black stallion with a braided mane — and opened the car door.

"Thank you, Somersby." James Fairleigh stepped out of the car in simple silk morning suit with grey waistcoat with matching pocket triangle, gloves, and spats, and began the ritual unpacking of his brass-and-leather-bound binoculars. He then took his place at the table, raised his binoculars, and panned slowly across the course until reaching a big blurry smiling obstacle.

"Teddy." Fairleigh lowered the spyglass. "Won't you join me? I should be most appreciative of your impressions of the first two races. I was unavoidably detained at a fitting at my collar-makers."

"What ho, Fairleigh. Don't mind if I do." Teddy pirouetted into a second card chair that Somersby prepared in the moment, informed by valet clairvoyance.

"You're looking marvellous, if it needs be said," charmed Fairleigh. "You put me in mind of Emil Adam's portrait of Kingcsem, the most successful mare in the history of the sport."

"It's this outfit." Teddy looked down at her country tweed

jacket and breeches. "I have a sequin shimmy dress that makes me look exactly like Man o' War."

Fairleigh raised a just-a-moment finger and said to his valet, "The '19 Heidsieck, I think, Somersby — we have a guest." Somersby issued a subtle eyebrow of self-reproach — the valet equivalent of slapping his forehead — and returned to the icebox in the car boot for a more seemly vintage.

Teddy slid Fairleigh a sly side-eye. "You should know, by the way, that I know your secret... Jimmy Fairly."

"What secret?"

"That one." Teddy gestured behind her at the secret which had just passed. "I know — it was easily missed. It's the sort of reveal that wants tudor trumpets or a crash of cymbals, but orchestration is so difficult in the country, don't you find?"

"Do you know, Teddy, what the most valuable currency is in the odds-making business?"

"I would guess currency."

"It's information, Teddy." Fairleigh raised his spyglass and aimed it at the paddock. "A bob's worth of tattle will fetch a pound on the odds market, but there's an important exception to this equation..."

"Relevancy?" proposed Teddy. "I can't imagine my bookie would give me much for the news that my postman's name is Mailer, delightful as that may be."

"Two exceptions." Fairleigh lowered his binoculars. "The information also must be reasonably exclusive."

"You're saying that everyone knows that you're Jimmy Fairly, gentleman odds-maker? Oh, thank you, Somersby."

"I thought everyone did," confessed Jimmy-James. "However it appears that you didn't, so who knows?

"Well, I won't say I'm not disappointed — I was very much looking forward to your stunned reaction and vain attempts to pry out of me how I worked it out." Teddy consoled herself with half her allotment of champagne.

"Please tell me how you worked it out?"

"No, it's too late. Thank you, but the moment is past." Teddy swirled her champagne through the pain. "Saves us scads of time, though. You know Oy Roy?"

"He's difficult to miss."

"That he is. I assume you also know about his difficulties with the mysterious sweet little old grey-haired tout and disqualified long shots."

"Mister Roy's problems are my problems." Fairleigh handed his binoculars to Somersby such that he might give full attention to spreading his napkin on his lap. "Just on a considerably larger scale."

"So I'm given to understand." Teddy tucked her napkin into her necklace. "All the other bookies lay off their extra risk with you, and you in turn divide it up among all the other bookies."

"Which is normally a smoothly operating insurance scheme, for the benefit of all. However, this notorious little old lady has introduced chaos. She seems to have targeted Oy Roy, who has in turn raised and broadened his hedge bets on longer odds horses which I, consequently, have difficulty laying off. This means I must offer even longer odds, or refuse Oy Roy's hedges, which would drive him out of business."

"But then, as often as not, these horses are disqualified," pointed out Teddy. "So you don't have to pay out."

Teddy and Fairleigh paused to allow Somersby a moment to serve the peeled Algarve pimentos, slowed marginally by a clogged balsamic vinegar syringe.

"That would be very convenient, if I knew which horses were going to be disqualified — would you like Somersby to slice your caper for you? That scalpel is an antique."

"I think I'll manage. I'll let you know if I get in trouble."

"The problem is the right information in the wrong hands." Fairleigh held up his pimento, as a handy symbol for information. "A white-haired old lady is touting winners to Oy Roy's customers, and a mysterious punter is guessing the winner of almost every race on which he bets with Jimmy Fairly's leg men."

"Jimmy Fairly has a psychic customer too?" Throwing caution to the wind, Teddy ate her caper whole.

"We do."

"It's not a little old lady is it?"

"A short man in an obvious disguise, apparently." Fairleigh sipped his 1920 Valmer but, in his agitated state, it might just as well have been a 1925 Bougros. "This is what my leg men tell me. Like Mister Roy's old lady, my diminutive in stage whiskers is targeting only myself and only certain racecourses, once again making it difficult to lay off the risk."

"Oy Roy thinks it's a conspiracy."

"It's difficult to imagine such a confluence of circumstances occurring by chance." Fairleigh tested his tweezers as Somersby served the individually-stuffed peas. "Do you know the second best thing to have, if you don't have information?"

"Of course," said Teddy. "An alibi."

"If you don't have information, Teddy, the next best thing is the appearance that you do."

"We work in very different sectors of the economy, Jimmy." Teddy, perhaps unwittingly and perhaps to illustrate a point, dropped her stuffed green pea into her champagne and drank it. "At Quillfeather Industries, our motto is stout denial — I can't tell you how many times I've been saved long and tedious explanations by a talent for saying 'To which penguin do you refer, Constable?' with convincing verisimilitude."

"If a bookmaker appears to know something, then others will want to know it, too," explained Fairleigh, "and they'll tell him what they know, hoping for a tip. Oy Roy spends all his time with jockeys and stable lads and other bookies, and so he has a reputation for being informed, but now this little old lady is selling winners and Oy doesn't even know which horses she's picked until the punters come to collect. Oy's in the dark and what's worse everyone knows it, so he has less currency to spend."

"And the only way to save his business is to work out which horses this little old lady is picking, or how she's doing it."

"Exactly correct, Teddy."

Somersby replaced the wine glasses to accommodate switching from the 1920 Valmer to a slightly colder 1920 Valmer, as accompaniment to the next course of estuary cockle carpaccio, with a Malabar peppercorn.

'Well, right oh, then." Teddy took up her cockle tongs. "Any tips on how that might be done? My first instinct is to loiter at the track, disguised as some knitting, but of course we're looking for a specific little old lady."

"You do it, Teddy, by finding the short man in the beard."

"Novel approach," toasted Teddy. "You think they're related?"

Fairleigh spoke distractedly as he lined up his peppercorn

mallet. "If you can work out how this bearded gentleman is picking winners, Teddy, I'll tell you how Oy's little old lady is picking hers."

"Just a tick — you know?"

"Of course I know, Teddy. I've known who she was since before she started selling tips."

"Spiffing." Teddy finished her quarter ounce of chablis and held up the thimble and a smile to Somersby. "Who is she?"

"Information, as I believe I already mentioned, Teddy, is currency. Don't you like your radish?"

"Is that what that is? I thought Somersby had lost a cufflink."

"It's peeled and glazed with Belizean agave. You just can't get Panamanian at this time of year."

"Oh, of course. Barribault's has ceased glazing their peeled radishes entirely, don't you know." Teddy crunched her radish. "What makes you think I can solve the mystery of the short beardy chap if you can't?"

"Tilden tells me it's what you do."

"You can't go by Stilts," dismissed Teddy with a wave of her mayonnaise dipper. "He's in love with me."

"He says that most men you know are in love with you."

"There you go. Can't trust any of them."

"You can trust me, Teddy."

"Oh, I know — I mean to say, if you can't trust a chap on whose shaved, uncooked limpet you've grown fat, there's not much hope for humanity." Sealing the deal, Teddy hand rolled her cockle carpaccio around its peppercorn, tossed the result into the air and caught it expertly on her mouth. "What about the epidemic of disqualifications? Who are you extorting into sorting that out?"

"It stands to reason, Teddy, that once we've identified the gentlemen who are second-guessing Jimmy Fairly, we'll know who's rigging the disqualifications."

"Think they're connected, do you?"

"I feel quite certain, Teddy, that all of these events are part of a single plot — a vengeance against the entire racing industry."

CHAPTER NINE

In which are scrutinised Marshpool's references.

THE NICEST, most luxurious guest rooms at Middleditch Castle are in the towers. Composed of two bedrooms and a communicating ensuite salon, they occupy fully half the surface of a tower floor, with doors giving onto Juliet balconies on two walls. They're kitted out in loving clutter, with antique tack and gear on the walls and mantles, along with paintings of horses representing an astonishingly broad spectrum of talents for painting horses. The furniture is fittingly unfitting — enormous oak four-posters and daintily complicated wardrobes, *écritoires*, and occasionals, and unevenly inflated leather club chairs. In brief, the guest rooms at Middleditch Castle are tremendously difficult to search.

The prowler was just realising how difficult it is to search three large, cluttered rooms, each positively tumbling with what seemed to him in the moment a million places to hide a horse, never mind the comparatively small parcel he sought, particularly when working to an unknowable but certainly tight deadline. The search was not, by even the most charitable analysis, methodical. He opened half the drawers of the writing desk before abandoning it as too obvious. This inspired him to check the least obvious places he could imagine, only to discover or, really, recall, that he had no imagination. He looked up the chimney and behind the equine portraits and under a rug and beneath the pillows, which he also took up and scrunched.

Surreptitiously searching a room is biliously stressful, if one is unused to this sort of thing, and this aspect was only compounded by a happy skirl from the crowd as the fourth race — the Middleditch Farrier's Four Furlongs for Any Horse Shoed by Middleditch Farrier's — came to a thrilling conclusion. It only served to remind the prowler that time was inexorably passing.

So it's just as well that he didn't know that he was being watched.

"What ho, Marshpool."

The butler, who had been endeavouring to pick the lock of a steamer trunk with a letter opener, launched the blade into the ceiling, where it stuck.

"No." By his tone, it sounded as though Marshpool meant this as a sort of blanket denial. He turned, slowly, in almost a complete circle before seeing Teddy in the open doorway of the west wall bedroom, leaning against the jamb.

"No, what?" wondered Teddy.

"No..." Marshpool gazed up at the letter opener, still quivering in the ceiling beam. "What was the question, again, Miss?"

"What ho, I believe."

"Oh."

"Want to stand by your answer?"

Marshpool reflected for an unproductive moment before deciding on, "Yes," spoken with a decided lack of conviction.

"What are you looking for?"

"Looking, Miss?" Marshpool pronounced the word as though it was unfamiliar to him. He glanced around the salon for inspiration. "That. Them, I mean to say. His Lordship's specs."

"You're looking for Lord Bitterbrook's pince-nez."

"Yes, Miss." Marshpool seized on this lifesaver. "His Lordship sent me for them."

"Those pince-nez there, on the writing desk."

Teddy and Marshpool regarded the unusually ornate spectacles, with damascene frames and chatelaine joined by a filament chain.

"Yes, Miss."

"And you thought they might be in that steamer trunk, did you?"

"Yes, Miss... I mean to say... yes, Miss."

Another cheer echoed across the gulley from the racecourse.

"Coming up on lunch, isn't it, Marshpool?"

"Oh, yes, Miss." Again, Marshpool grasped at what he saw as a lifeline — Teddy, he hoped, was hungry, and anxious to be on her way.

"You don't think you ought to be limbering up the gonging arm, then?"

Marshpool, having now entirely exhausted his armoury of yeses and nos, issued an entirely unconvincing laugh, transliterated here, poorly, as "ah... ha." Doesn't at all do it justice.

"You must miss the cannon," blindsided Teddy, as she began to tour the room.

"Ah... ha."

"You were at Handsome Hall prior to coming to Middleditch, were you not, Marshpool?" Teddy opened the top left drawer of the *écritoir*, wherein she found the key to the steamer trunk. "Where, I believe you mentioned, you were in charge of the dinner gong."

Marshpool recalled saying this, now, and saw, incorrectly, no reason to not stand by it.

"Yes, Miss."

"Handsome Hall is the country seat of Lord Stibling, who is my uncle or cousin or some such thing. When in residence, he insists on announcing dinner, every evening, with a live cannon."

"Not really."

"There was a brief hiatus, one summer I was there with my cousin Anty, while they tried to work out who kept packing the cannon with fireworks and purple paint, but yes, really."

"Fancy that." The butler nodded pensively, hoping against all probability to move the conversation onto the theme of paint.

"Where were you really before coming here, Marshpool?" Teddy opened the steamer trunk.

"I don't remember..." attempted Marshpool. "I mean to say, I was... at a place... you haven't heard of."

"You were in service with Lord Bitterbrook, weren't you Marshpool?" Teddy had to speak up a bit now, as her head was in the steamer trunk. "And you're still in his service." She resurfaced with a fur muffler. "You're his spy. That's how Lord Sticky knows about the Irish reels on violin when the only person outside of immediate family who should know anything about it is you."

"Lord Bitterbrook... Bitterbrook... " Marshpool rocked on his heels and searched the skies for some distant recollection of the name.

"You really have no talent for this at all, Marshpool." Teddy regarded herself in the wall mirror, wearing the fur muffler as a makeshift beard. "Which causes me to conclude that Sticky chose you not because you were well suited to espionage but because he could oblige you to do it, regardless."

Teddy returned the muffler to the trunk and then put her head into the wardrobe.

"And that's also why you're searching his room — you're looking for the evidence he has of something you've done..." Teddy withdrew from the wardrobe, empty-handed. "Something that can be proven with evidence that can be easily transported and hidden in a guest bedroom..."

Marshpool smiled weakly and shifted his feet, like a guilty man in the dock, listening to the charges as they're read out to the court.

Teddy tapped her chin meditatively and squinted appraisingly at Marshpool. "Upstairs maid?"

Marshpool studied his shoes. "Parlour."

"You wrote her letters, exposing yourself to a breach of promise claim, and Lord Bitterbrook paid the girl off, but he keeps the letters and the threat that the suit could be brought at any time."

Marshpool issued a rapid guilty plea of a nod.

"What made you think he would bring the letters to Middleditch?" asked Teddy as she wandered the room, picking things up and testing their heft.

"I know he has, Miss." Marshpool also wandered the room, but only with his eyes. His feet remained cold and numb. "His Lordship gives me one letter for any information he regards as useful."

"That's the second time today I've encountered information used as literal currency," observed Teddy. "I've searched Sticky's room, that leaves only Lady Bitterbrook's." Teddy led the way into the second bedroom. Marshpool followed as far as the door.

"If I might take the liberty, Miss... what are *you* looking for?"

"I'm not entirely sure, frankly, Marshman. A false beard would be ideal. Have you ever known His Lordship to sport false whiskers?"

"No, Miss."

"Doesn't mean he doesn't, though, as a disguise to keep people finding out he bets on or against his own horses."

"Very true, Miss."

Teddy could see in an instant that there was no place to hide any number of letters in Lady Olivia's room, so she occupied herself with mismatching the ensembles in the armoire.

"Well, Marshminder, it appears as though you'll just have to continue spying, at least for the moment. What is it?"

Marshpool had taken on the pained expression and posture associated with the exact moment a bad oyster makes itself known.

"His Lordship is expecting a report — this afternoon."

"So, tell him there's nothing to report. Tell him what Lord Markham had for breakfast. It was kippers, in case you've forgotten."

"Lord Bitterbrook knows it's not true."

"It is true, though," differed Teddy. "Plus a fried egg. Runny."

"I mean he knows that I have a very big secret to report."

"Have you a big secret to report?"

Marshpool could only nod again.

"What big secret?" asked Teddy.

The butler bent closer to Teddy and spoke in confidential tones. "Lord Markham placed a bet on Chockit Rockit to win Cheveley."

"How do you know that, or, put much more in line with what I wish I'd just said, what makes you think that?"

"I was there when he told Her Ladyship to place the bet."

"And how does Lord Bitterbrook come to know that you have a big secret?"

"I told him." Marshpool returned to the study of his shoes. "I asked him if I could have all the letters back if I gave him something big, regarding a horse."

"Oh, good show, Marshpool — I hope if there's ever another war you'll be good enough to spy for the enemy."

"I didn't know how grave the consequences were, at the time," agonised the butler. "And now he expects me to tell him this afternoon."

"A secret about a horse."

"Yes, Miss."

"So, tell him a secret about a horse," proposed Teddy. "Just not that secret. That secret is a secret secret."

"I don't have another secret to tell him."

"Make something up, Marshly..." Teddy, reflecting on recent history and the look of pure panic on the butler's face, reconsidered. "Oh, right, no, don't try making something up. It could be literally fatal. All right, then tell him something true."

"But it's got to be a secret."

"No, I know that..." Teddy walked to the window and looked out at the paddock, where Mister Yardpole was discussing strategy with what he thought was a jockey but was, in fact, a member of the boys' choir. "Tell him about Chockit Rockit's cousin."

"He knows about Overdraught," complained Marshpool. "He belongs to the Bitterbrook stable."

"That's the secret. There's another cousin — by Chockit Rockit's uncle and a direct descendent of Kingcsem, the most successful mare in the history of the sport. Her name is Piccadilly Larking and in three separate trials, under almost all conditions, she beat Chockit Rockit by never less than eight lengths. She's at a stable outside London and, if and when this scandal blows over, Lord Markham is going to buy her and bring her here."

"What stable?" asked Marshpool, visibly encouraged.

"I'm not telling you that — you'd just tell Sticky and then he'd buy Piccadilly Larking out from under poor Uncle Markham."

"He's going to ask."

"That's why I'm not telling you."

"Oh, right." Marshpool marshalled his thoughts. "That's probably for the best."

"Do you want to bring Sticky's specs?" Teddy nodded at the pince-nez on the writing desk. "In case you need to explain why you were in this room?"

"Those aren't really his, Miss. They belong to Lady Brimble, and Lord Bitterbrook can't see with them at all. He borrowed them to lend tone to a meeting with his solicitor and neglected to return them." Marshpool surveyed the room. "Why, Miss? Do you think he'll know someone was here?"

"You never know what subtle differences he might notice — a door or drawer left ajar, a curtain out of place, a letter-opener stuck in the ceiling."

Marshpool's mood regressed visibly. He gazed at the ceiling and shook his head at it, as one marvelling at life's litany of trials.

"It doesn't matter," Sensing Marshpool's deteriorating state,

Teddy spoke comforting words in calm tones, "because I also apple-pied his bed. In any case, he'll forget all about it when you tell him about Piccadilly Larking."

'He'll want to know how I found out about her," realised Marshpool.

'So tell him — you heard it from me," Teddy advised. "Just stick to the truth, Middlemarsh, and you'll be fine. That's what I always do."

CHAPTER TEN

In which Stilts and Vicar Bittles, respectively and in their own time, fail to convey a powerful message, and Teddy takes note of a disturbing pattern.

"THAT'S WHAT YOU ALWAYS DO, TEDDY."

Stilts made this observation sound very much like a complaint from the back of a good-natured but almost entirely spiritless speckled mare named Dropcloth.

"I always do what, Stilts?" wondered Teddy, only slightly, from atop a good-natured palomino pony.

"You let your horse pick her own path." Stilts gestured, forwards and aft, at the path in question, which was a muddy stretch between hedgerow and a field of shoots of winter oat. A still afternoon fog floated above the Shropshire countryside, compounding a cosy contiguity between horse and hedgerow and field and forest, and imposing a calm, whispery quiet, like a misty great librarian.

"Not at all." Teddy patted the withers of her pony whose name, in keeping with her coat and comity, was Pal o' Mine. "We discussed it at length and settled on a full itinerary."

Stilts assumed a professorial demeanour or, he would have done, were he not fitted out entirely in hunting costume including, reading from bottom-left, patent leather knee boots, jodhpurs, crimson riding coat, white silk cravat, and short black satin topper. All this, tightly tailored, and the fact that Stilts was riding a speckled mare, gave him the appearance of the pole of a carousel horse.

"Riding, Theodora Quillfeather, is the very pinnacle, unimprovable meeting of man and nature. If you just let the horse have her way it becomes... well it becomes man *riding* nature. A very different thing — utilitarian and spare. One might as well take a bus."

"Precisely." Teddy held up her free hands. "I need to be at liberty to gesticulate. I have much to wildly gesture." She cast a careful connoitre over her shoulder at the trailing members of the party — Lady Bitterbrook, Vicar Bittles, and Lady Middleditch, riding three abreast. "There have been developments."

Stilts slowed his canter to match that of Pal o' Mine. "Did Oy Roy deliver already? I told you he could be trusted."

"It was Lady Lulu who bet on Chockit Rockit to win Cheveley."

"Ah ha!" Stilts processed this, aided by a cunning squint into the fog. "Oh, I say, that's actually rather mouldy, isn't it?"

"No, not really," judged Teddy. "At least not compared to the fact that Uncle Markham told her to place the bet."

Carried lightly on the still air was the tinny rattle of forced laughter, as Lady Lulu did the double duty of affecting levity at both the vicar's cuddly allegorising and the sharp edges which Lady Olivia employs in place of wit. Stilts and Teddy urged their horses from an amble to a canter, and the fog closed over them.

"Where does that put us, Teddy?" whispered Stilts.

"Certainly not greatly improved, but not necessarily any worse, so long as no one finds out that Lord Markham profited from Chockit Rockit's surprising win. And while you're keeping that secret, you can get back onto Oy Roy about how a horse who finished an embarrassing last, five races in a row, can win the next with six lengths of daylight between him and second place."

"He doesn't know, though, does he Teddy?" countered Stilts. "Oy Roy was sure it was the jockeys that held back Chockit Rockit, but you heard Pudge Hillock and Flat Milliken — they said it wasn't them. We're stymied."

Teddy smiled upwardly and indulgently at Stilts. "Is it possible that someone is telling porkies?"

"Teddy..." Stilts put a scandalised hand to a trusting heart, "...these men are jockeys."

"Nevertheless, the jockeys are key to it, that's a certainty, and the only hope that Uncle Markham has now is that we can prove that he didn't have anything to do with Chockit Rockit's remarkable turnaround."

"Even though he himself says that he did it," Stilts reminded Teddy. "With violins."

"And if he admits to that he'll be warned off for sure and for good, and Bitterbrook already knows it."

"Oh, I say, Teddy, look — a ditch." Stilts spoke of the shallow drain dividing the oat field from a newly ploughed hay field as though it was the heretofore undeclared eighth natural wonder. "Last one over's a spotted egg."

And with a tall-tenoured "Tally-ho" Stilts urged on Dropcloth, who trotted up to the ditch, had a drink of cold field water, and then stepped over onto the hay field. Teddy's horse crossed via the culvert.

"We'll look for a hedge. Much more motivating, hedges," promised Stilts. "How does Lord Bitterbrook already know that Lord Markham thinks he makes horses faster by playing them Irish reels on violin?"

"Marshpool told him."

"Why the devil did he do that?"

"Marshpool is Sticky's spy at Middleditch."

"Why that blighted blighter," miffed Stilts. "I assume he's been escorted from the premises."

"No, the poor jelly — he's being blackmailed." Teddy once again confirmed that the ladies and the minister were trailing in the fog, "He used to be in service with the Bitterbrooks, where he wrote compromising letters to the parlour maid. Lord Sticky is using them to make Mushpool do his bidding."

"Why that blighting blighted blighter."

"He won't reveal anything else of value, and his very presence proves that Bitterbrook is trying to incriminate Uncle Markham."

"Unless he's installed spies in all his rivals' houses," suggested Stilts, gazing into the fog for — and finding — inspiration; "He does seem to go through rather a lot of butlers. Op! Here we go…"

Stilts chirruped his horse into a jaunty gallop towards a copse of brooding cyprus, drooping and dripping with ambient wet. The trees bordered and gated the hedgerow where it separated the field from a rough road, and it was over this modest hurdle that Stilts determined to build a bond with Dropcloth. Horse and rider disappeared into the branches, a certain amount of not unanticipated oofing and wahooing was heard, and Stilts' top hat was slingshot out of the thicket by a cyprus branch.

"Took it a little high." Stilts stooped out from beneath the tangle of branches. "Which, by the way young Theodora, is the sort of enthusiasm you just don't get from a bus."

Stilts took up his hat and they found their way through a natural passage to the road where, to Stilts, Dropcloth appeared to be reviewing her form while to Teddy she appeared to be looking for Stilts. She was, in fact, wondering what if any of the hedge was edible.

Stilts heaved back into the saddle and the cantilever effect caused Dropcloth to dance two paces sideways.

"Shall we take the hedge again? I feel that Dropcloth knows where she went wrong."

"I think she does too." Teddy appraised Stilts, tall in the saddle, wearing his muddy top hat, and effectively doubling the height of the horse. "You don't think wind resistance might be a factor?"

"I have very aquiline features, Teddy," said Stilts with cool aplomb. "You know who you sound like?"

"Who?"

"Well, in point of fact, no one person in particular — just about everyone in the entire blinking industry. Mister Yardpole, for one, every jockey I've ever met, Oy Roy, James Fairleigh... Lord Markham won't even let me exercise Spoons, never mind Chockit Rockit."

"I'm sure it's nothing personal, Stilts."

"I assure you it isn't, Theodora — it's blanket prejudice against the tall."

"Well, I appreciate you, Stilts. In fact, later, you can pull a letter opener out of a ceiling beam for me. In the meantime, though..." Teddy gestured with an incline of the head towards the vicar and the ladies, who'd just clopped out of the mist. "We have much to discuss which is for your ears and those of Dropcloth and Pal o' Mine only."

The horses dropped into a rhythmic canter down the road towards Middleditch High Street.

"So, you'll get Oy Roy back onto the question of how Chockit Rockit was nobbled and denobbled," continued Teddy. "And you can assure him that I'm closing in on his little old lady track tout."

"Are you?"

"Don't tell Oy this, but Jimmy Fairly says he knows who she is."

"Oh, I say, jolly good. Did you ask him who it was?"

"Oh, pox." Teddy slapped her forehead. "Completely slipped my mind. If you'd been there to taste the green tapenade served on a half a Persian pistachio you'd have been distracted too."

"Sarcastic reparté only makes me love you more, Teddy," Stilts warned her. "Did he tell you how to scout out the tout?"

"No, but he says he will do, just as soon as I tell him who's doing the same to him."

"Is someone doing the same to Jimmy Fairly?" The horses, wondering something altogether more immediate and practical, came to a stop where the farm road met High Street Middleditch. "Which way?"

"That way, I think, into town — we still have much to discuss before the others catch up."

"Lady Llewella, I'll merely note without commentary, is riding Spoons," observed Stilts. "A valuable, delicate, perfectly-tuned instrument, and she's riding him through fields of unknown and uneven aspect."

"Supposing you were going to pass comment, Stilts, what might it be?"

"Only that I'm not even allowed to take Spoons once around Middleditch Racecourse, is all," said Stilts with admirable restraint.

"He's her horse, Stilts, and they love each other," pointed out Teddy. "And, when mounted, Aunty Lulu and Spoons can still fit under a stable door. Now, let us hie for the high street, Stilts, the vicar and his devoted following are closing fast."

Teddy needn't have concerned herself, for Lady Llewella and Lady Olivia were at least as keen to keep their conversation with the vicar private as Teddy was hers with Stilts. Indeed, given a choice in the matter, either lady would have been happy for either other lady to be swallowed up by a sinkhole.

However Lady Lulu, as has been observed, was riding Spoons, and was consequently in winning and winsome spirit. From this, she drew the strength to issue a lady-like laugh precisely on the point of every perceived punctuation from the vicar, and to maintain a steady titter whenever Lady Olivia finished speaking or during moments of dead air. Riding and communing with

Spoons, a direct descendent of her warmest girlish memories, also gave Lady Lulu the courage to get past the fact that, in a rash dash to match Lady Olivia on their outing, she'd added a feather boa to her riding habit and wore a pillbox fascinator with a partridge feather for a combined effect not unlike Chicken, apart from the nervous laugh.

Lady Olivia Bitterbrook displayed mere apathy (despite being, obviously, tremendously pathy) and in fact by all outward appearances she had forgotten that Lady Llewella had joined the ride — only addressing herself to the vicar, for instance, or interrupting Lady Lulu frequently, or commenting how pleasant it was to have Vicar Bittles to herself, for a change. Lady Bitterbrook didn't wear jewellery or a hat, but she did wear brocade matador trousers and a jacket designed and hand-made by Mariano Fortuny, as a prototype costume for an as-yet unnamed opera by Ravel. She rode a nutmeg-coloured horse named Muscade, which is French for nutmeg.

Vicar Bittles, bestrode a brown and burgundy brindle-striped, untried two-year-old colt named Pocket Change, wore his country vicar riding outfit, which was also his country vicar everything else outfit, two scarves (each one a gift from the ladies), and an air of pacific patience.

"You know, ladies, before I came to Middleditch I was parson at Saint Mary's in Little Boring, in Essex. Among my happy duties was the organisation of the flower arranging contest, held, owing to a scarcity of diversions in Little Boring, on a bi-monthly basis."

"Ha ha," punctuated Lady Lulu.

"Whatever did you do for flowers in winter?" wondered Lady Olivia.

"Substitutions were found..." The vicar smiled handsomely at the recollection. "Twigs mainly, and I recall some tremendously ingenious arrangements of mushrooms and bark."

"Ha ha," replied Lady Lulu adding, as there appeared to be an opportunity to score a point, "ha."

"Don't you find Middleditch utterly dreary in winter, Vicar?" Olivia flicked a dismissive wave at the haze and waves of the silent tableau of Shropshire farm country. "And spring. And summer, of course. I'm sure that Lord Bitterbrook could find you something in the south-east, if you don't object to working closely with the authorities at Canterbury."

Lulu laughed just a half a pitch over too high. "Of course, here in Middleditch we have racing the year round."

"Yes, quite…" steered Vicar Bittles. "Tremendously ingenious flower arrangements indeed, and certainly among the most baroque were those of Mrs Sealy and Mrs Hollyhandler, ever such delightful ladies, and very close neighbors…"

"You know, Vicar, my husband and I are establishing our own stable," off-handed Lady Olivia. "Exclusive to only the finest thoroughbreds…" she lowered her voice, but not very much, "…I shall provide some very intriguing details, when we're at our leisure to speak freely."

"Very close neighbors, indeed." Vicar Bittles spoke now in his sermon voice. "In time, though, the contentious nature of competitive flower-arranging began to come between them as, indeed, it did the entire village of Little Boring, as Mrs Sealy and Mrs Hollyhandler, I'm afraid to say, lobbied their neighbours for support."

"Is Pocket Change to your liking, Vicar?" idled Lady Olivia. "He's one of ours, you know. Until his first race, Lord Bitterbrook and I are keeping him a secret here in Middleditch because it's so very, very remote."

"These jealousies, you see, will spread like a flu," continued the diagnosis of Vicar Bittles.

"That's so very true, Vicar," agreed Lulu with a solemn chuckle. "Perhaps later, when we've freed ourselves of other… ah-hahaha… commitments, you'd care for a tour of the stables. We're training up some remarkable entries for this Flat season, and I think I can offer you some tips, ah ha, right from the horse's mouth."

Battling temptation on all sides, Vicar Bittles continued the prophetic homily. "In time, hostilities grew to the point that Mrs Sealy and Mrs Hollyhandler were accusing one another of vandalising their respective gardens, sheds, and even their finished arrangements…" the vicar added a theatrical tremolo and assumed the countenance of one staring into the depths, "…in broad daylight… in the church basement."

Olivia nodded approvingly. Lulu laughed nervously.

"Suspicions grew deeper and darker," thundered the cleric, "and Mrs Sealy and Mrs Hollyhandler took to spying on each other, employing agents, setting traps, hiding for hours in rain barrels, but neither could ever catch the other in the act. It appeared that the ladies had perverted their gifts for creativity and ingenuity to clandestine sabotage."

"Yes, most instructive," said Olivia with admiration.

"Ehm, no, you see, I counselled Mrs Sealy and Mrs Hollyhandler, and suggested that they could accomplish so much more if they only worked together," preached the vicar.

"And... did they?" doubted Olivia.

"They most certainly did. They discovered that the sabotage wasn't being done by their respective rivals at all, but by deputations from the entire town of Little Boring. Indeed, the most creative mischief was perpetrated by Messers Sealy and Hollyhandler, who, ironically, demonstrated quite admirable team spirit."

As the vicar squandered his talent for drawing out charitable humours, Stilts and Teddy stopped in front of proof that, at least sometimes, it was worth a try.

By 1928, Saint Paul's and All Angels church in Middleditch had been churching in Middleditch for over a thousand years. Much of it was original, including the cracked, stacked, rude stone walls, but much more of it had been recently refurbished or refinished or replaced, such as a roof of new shale, a 408 pipe organ with six manuals and 312 stops (including a Gemshorn specially tuned to the unique acoustics of Saint Paul's and All Angels), and most of the glass in the rosette window. Three rooms and a second floor had been added to the parish hall, accommodating a kitchen, tea room, library, crèche, and billiards room (an innovation which, on its own, tripled attendance at the bake sales). A bandstand now stood in the park, next to the new cricket pitch, which is where the fountain used to be. The fountain (with the lambs all redone in Banbury marble) had been moved to the freshly cobbled carriage court at the entrance to the church. The same entrance was now plated in etched copper.

"Blimey," observed Teddy. "Has Saint Paul's and All Angels always had a concierge?"

"He's mainly a groom. Now they've finished the livery barn, a lot of parishioners arrive on horseback." Stilts appraised the church grounds with vacant approval, and then expanded his blessing to Middleditch High Street when he, or at the very least, his eyebrows, had an epiphany. "So, in sum, Teddy, to keep all this from packing up and moving directly down the tubes, we have to find out how Chockit Rockit won Cheveley against all odds."

"Yes."

"And to do that we have to find this little old lady who's touting Oy Roy's punters."

"Yes."

"And to do that we have to find a short chap with a greasepaint beard who's doing the same thing to Jimmy Fairly — is that it?"

"No," said Teddy. "I mean to say, yes, but it's not all of it. We also have to stop a trackwide conspiracy to disqualify selected longshot winners, get Marshpool's letters back from Lord Bitterbrook, and work out why Spoons is underperforming before his first race on Monday."

"Right." Stilts removed his hat such that he might scratch his head, but then put it back in place when he realised that he might need his fingers for counting. "That's Chockit Rockit's impossible performance at Cheveley, Oy Roy's clairvoyant little old lady, Jimmy Fairly's equally psychic beardo, suspect disqualifications, Marshpool's letters to the parlour maid, and what's this about Spoons?"

"He's performing poorly."

"Just nerves, I expect." Stilts nodded knowingly. "I'll have a word with him, explain it's only one race. There'll be others."

"That's just it, there won't be," doomspoke Teddy. "Mister Yardpole tells me that Spoons' first race is a claim race, the conditions of which are that every horse but the winner is claimed for a fixed price, less two hundred pounds per pound taken off the handicap."

"Lord Markham can just place a claim for his own horse," offhanded Stilts. "Happens all the time."

"He'd be only one of an unknowable many, and the claimants are drawn by lot."

"Oh, right. That's true, isn't it?"

"The only chance is for Spoons to win. The winner is auctioned off publicly, and Uncle Markham can bid the national debt if he likes — he's buying his own horse, in the end."

Stilts reflected on this just a stitch longer than would have been ideal, before wondering out loud, "Whyever would Spoons' first race be a claim race?"

Returning briefly to the theme of the spectacle of Saint Paul's and All Angels church, it was this striking presence which had arrested Teddy and Stilts for the majority of the above exchange, such that they hadn't noticed that Lady Olivia, Vicar Bittles, and, above all, Lady Llewella had ridden out of the fog and into convenient eavesdropping distance.

"Spoons is running in a claim race?" Lady Llewella regarded Teddy with big, baleful eyes which she then settled slowly onto Spoons, issuing, even by her standards, a tinny and toneless "Ha… ha."

CHAPTER ELEVEN

Featuring foreign fields and espionage and the reformative power of temperance.

BROMFORD BRIDGE RACECOURSE is close enough to Middleditch for many of the stable's supporters to make a day of it. A special rail service is laid on for race days, in fact, and anyone from the village who wanted to cheer on some two dozen local favourites running in the Bromford Bridge Good Friday meet, most of whom they knew personally, needed only take the regular service to Shrewsbury, then the London Omnibus, changing at Kidderminster for Birmingham where, two refreshing hours later, they'd be on the city bus to Aston Street, from which they could avail themselves of the eight-minute Bromford Bridge Race Day Special Train, or just walk over the bridge.

And that's just what roughly half the village of Middleditch did. This wasn't their home ground, though — Bromford Bridge was an official track with meets sanctioned by the Jockey Club — and so the Middleditch day-trippers banded together, in large part, and left the unicycles and pantomime horses and home-made fascinators at home. Best to not be too conspicuous, was the general reasoning, when visiting foreign parts.

The weather, as it so often does in springtime, betrayed and belayed everyone's planning and preparation with a calm, clear, cloudless, and cool flawless day for racing. A thousand galoshes, brollies, slickers, and all-season kerchiefs were toted about in listless, unspoken optimism for a change in the weather.

Bromford's perfect mile was formed of two long, parallel straights joined at the ends by short curves. It was a course for jockeys and for horses, in this regard, and also because it offered little for anyone else. A charmingly Lilliputian grandstand stood as far from the entrance to the park as could be reasonably managed, at the end of the muddiest path that could be provided, and it had an excellent view of the finish, for those who wanted to see which horse won, and a broad selection of Silver Ring bookies, for those who wanted to care which horse won.

Consequently, the untamed terrain outside the gates, formed of urban grasslands and mud lots and commanding a view of Birmingham's famously scenic warehouse district, was the unofficial hospitality zone. This is where the Middleditch tea ladies set out their tent, across from a beer garden commissioned by the Middleditch Society of Blokes Who Never Like to be Too Far From a Pint. There was also a solicitor's advice card table, offering a free consultation, a produce stand featuring eggs and local cheeses, and, representing the tentacles of the business empire of Sinjin Lord Ashby, several men selling helium-filled balloons.

Teddy had travelled by carriage behind the parade of horse boxes from Middleditch Stables to the rough stalls of Bromford Bridge. She arrived fully an hour before the first fixture and so she idled by the paddock, watching a stable lad lead Chockit Rockit, prancing and shot through with undirected energy, to his stall. This left Chockit Rockit's trailer empty. After a quick but casual 360 degree scan of the immediate area, Teddy approached the box, knocked lightly on the door, and whispered, "There will be rain in Northumberland tomorrow."

This was followed by the sound of spirited rustling of canvas, straw, and introvert, and a hoarse, "Eh?"

'It's the secret signal, 'There will be rain in Northumberland tomorrow,'" explained Teddy. "The correct response is, 'Eh?'"

Aunty Azalea peered over the trailer door. "Was I meant to have known that?"

"Not explicitly," admitted Teddy, "but who else is going to say 'There will be rain in Northumberland tomorrow' to an empty horse box? All ready?"

"No." Azalea's head dipped away, like a shy hand-puppet. "I think I can manage from in here."

"You're going to do a thorough census of all the short, bearded chaps at the races from inside a horse trailer?"

"And under a blanket. Yes."

Teddy pulled the door open. "You'll be fine, Agent A. Got up like that you might just as well be a pantomime horse. I guarantee that no one is going to talk to you."

Teddy and her aunt had invested creativity and honest labour into the costume in equal measure, and now Azalea's hair was tied rigidly back and powdered to make complete her partial grey, her overwashed pewter-coloured dress began in choking lace beneath her chin from which it rumpled to the floor in formless muslin, and she wore a plain chain and cross of the size and style favoured by The Order of Cistercians of the Strict Observance. In case the point was somehow missed, she carried a generous stack of temperance literature.

"No one will even make eye contact." Teddy, to eliminate any remaining risk that she might be confused for her aunt, wore a belted trench coat and wide-brimmed hat. "We shall proceed separately. I'm going to surveil the bookies, betting heavily to avoid suspicion. You install yourself at the tea tent — you like the tea ladies — and take careful note of any men under, say, five foot four acting suspiciously — applying or removing false whiskers, for example. If anyone tries to talk to you, just show him that tract on 'Whisky — Drinking the Devil's Bath Water'."

The Saint Paul's and All Angels Boys Choir had set up, quite cleverly, round the bend of the ad-hoc gallery from the beer garden, so that by the time a chap saw them it was too late — he was in range of a fully armed and deployed *All Things Bright and Beautiful.*

One such punter named Collin, a genial shipping clerk on the rise in Birmingham's textiles trade, stepped into the trap and stuck, and so was obliged to remove his cap and smile blinkingly through *Saint Matthew Passion,* Vicar Bittles conducting. Collin had difficulty fully appreciating the performance, because he was anxious to institute his betting system, which had been in development for some days. His plan was to walk the length of the far straight, taking note of all the odds offered by all the bookies, and then walk back again, taking note of any that had changed. That was, in fact, the extent of Collin's system, but he had an instinct that this exercise was bound to turn up a hidden gem, and it was certain to be more reliable than his previous system of betting on the horse with the second-longest odds in every race.

Collin's efforts to move along — sidling slowly and pretending that he recognised someone just the other side of the choir — were foiled and even reversed by Vicar Bittles, who with practiced frequency would turn his beguiling benevolence on the consequently captive audience.

Then, just when Collin was sure that he'd identified and occupied a blind spot from which to effect an escape, he found himself fenced in by propriety.

"Lovely, isn't it?"

Collin looked down. Next to and roughly the height of his shoulder was a sweet little old grey-haired lady.

'Yes," he sighed, resignedly. "Very lovely. Makes me sometimes wish I'd..."

"Shropshire Lass in the first."

"Hm?"

"Shropshire Lass is going to win the first race, and is currently being offered at twelve to one," said the sweet little old etc., without taking her eyes off the choir, and without changing her tone from that which she'd used when she said 'lovely, isn't it?'

"How do you...?"

The sweet little old tout regarded Collin with the steely eye of cold commerce.

'Oh, right oh." Collin resumed the uneasy pretense that he was simply one of two innocent civilians, appreciating a very promising rendition of *They That Go Down to the Sea in Ships*.

"It's Chockit Rockit by nine laughing lengths."

Stilts announced the results of the fourth race from the wrong side of the track, nearer the entrance to the park and the beer garden and choir, but across from the grandstand and finish line. Stilts, however, rising above the crowd like a periscope, was able to commentate the race to Teddy in real time.

It came to her as no surprise. The fourth race — The Worcester Bar Handicap Silver Bell — had appeared, from the sidelines, as two distinct races, superimposed. One race was eleven horses of roughly similar qualifications running Bromford Bridge Racecourse, and the other was Chockit Rockit on, apparently, a much shorter track.

Stilts lowered his binoculars. "Shall we claim fame and champagne in the Winners Circle, Tedds?"

Between races, narrow boards were laid across the track for the convenience of any funambulists prepared to teeter across to the inner circle, wherein were found the unsaddling and Winners Enclosures. Stilts, who was too tall to maintain his balance in a breeze but in any case liked the feel of honest course beneath his feet, trotted happily along next to the boards, stopping momentarily to let Teddy catch up and to take in the majesty of the track, stretching four flat furlongs in either direction, and to dream of a world in which a man is judged at least as much for his sportsmanship as for his inseam.

The Winners Enclosure was a flurry of unproductive activity. Champagne was uncorked and wasted or splashed into glasses from which no one drank. Flat waved to the grandstand and shook hands with the stewards and Lord Markham as a distraction from the champagne, which he denied himself between races, along with whisky, cigars, and punching policemen. The stable lad was trying to unsaddle Chockit Rockit, and Mister Yardpole was trying to remove what looked like buckshot from his left back hoof with a farrier pick, and the two men were perfectly cancelling one another out.

Teddy took up a glass of champagne and shook hands with Flat Milliken. "Well done, not falling off, and all that."

"It were a close run thing, too." The jockey shook his head at hard memories best left in the distant mire of the grandstand curve. "It's tight turns, is Bromford Bridge, and Chockit Rockit likes to take them close to the rail without slowing down. I think he might have sped up, in point of fact. If I hadn't leaned almost sideways into the bend and had that second crumpet for tea I'd have landed in the canal."

The stable lad, who was a grown man of 43 years in undersized overalls and two left Wellies, shared an empathetic grimace with Stilts, as will two tall men on the periphery of racing. Then he finally unsaddled Chockit Rockit, freeing Mister Yardpole to pop the last little lead pellet out of Chockit's back left hoof, and releasing him to step immediately into another pile of buckshot with his front right.

"Chockit Rockit seems to have returned fully to form," observed Teddy.

"And that's with a handicap of one stone six." Flat wobbled under the weight of his saddle as the stable lad heaved it onto his shoulder. "Which was the maximum for the race, all on account of his win at Cheveley."

"I noticed." Teddy held up her betting slip. "Best I could get was 2-5. Still, puts me up half a shilling on the day — buy you a glass of champers?"

"Mustn't touch a thing 'till I'm weighed in." Flat waved away temptation like a martyr, and limped off to the scales, and Teddy joined Stilts and Lord Markham.

"Thanks very much for the twenty quid, Your Lordship." Stilts, too, was displaying a betting slip.

"You put fifty pounds Chockit Rockit to win?" marvelled Teddy.

"Near as a sure thing I've seen all day," defended Stilts.

"You never know when he might return to past form," pointed out Teddy. "Remember what happened to Charlie the Wonder Horse."

"Ehm..." Stilts said it, but both men thought it.

"Charlie the Wonder Horse," Teddy reminded them. "Discovered on an alfalfa farm in Nevada and brought to Hollywood. The studios spent a fortune on singing and dancing lessons... comportment, diction, dressage... for two years he's the toast of the town — twenty-seven hit westerns in a row and one middling romantic comedy, endorsements for everything from cereal oats to porridge oats, hoofprints in the sidewalk in front of Grauman's Chinese Theatre — then he just... disappears."

"What happened?" wondered Stilts, despite years of acquaintance with Teddy's tales.

"Went back to pulling a plow," said Teddy. "Turned out he just missed the outdoors. At least, that's what he said in his memoirs."

"Ahh, but Chockit Rockit's win *was* a sure thing." Lord Markham squinted and tried and failed to raise one eyebrow, implying canny confidence. "I played him to sleep last night with *Drowsy Maggy.*"

"There you go." Stilts secured his betting slip inside his hat.

"How about you, Uncle Mark?" asked Teddy. "How much did you win?"

"I told you, Teddy, I never bet on my own horses."

"Yes, I know you *told* me that, Uncler — we're not discussing the things you say you do, we're talking about that which you actually do, such as laying a whacking great bet on Chockit Rockit to win Cheveley."

"I didn't."

"No, you got Aunty Lew to do it."

"That's right."

"You know it amounts to the same thing, don't you?"

"Does it?" Lord Markham screwed up the question into a kneaded squint, and focussed it on the middle field. After a few moments of this and a bit of helpful nodding, he said, "Oh, yes, I see what you mean. Oh dear."

"Does anyone else know?"

"I think your Aunty Lew might."

"Apart from her."

"I'm not sure... How did you find out?"

"Thumb screws," said Teddy. "Aunty Lew's a tough nut. Just don't tell anyone else, and stop betting on your own horses until this steward's inquiry is satisfactorily concluded, or at least until we figure out how Chockit Rockit was held so decisively back for five races."

"I've already explained that, Teddy."

"And don't tell anyone else about the Irish reels, either," warned Teddy. "We have it on very good authority that any such explanation will be received by the stewards as a flimsy guise for proper dirty work, like opera and balloons, only more so."

"I see." Lord Markham nodded gravely at the comparison. "What am I to do, Teddy?"

"Just carry on being adorably dotty," advised Teddy. "Speaking of which, why is Spoons registered for a claim race?"

"He isn't," said Lord Markham. "I still haven't done the paperwork. I must get round to it — the race is Monday."

"But why are you entering him in a claim race at all?"

"Why shouldn't I?"

"Because if he loses the race you'll lose him, and then Aunty Lew will poison your tea."

'That's just it, Teddy." Markham spoke with lolly-eyed sincerity. "In a claim race, we set our own handicap weight — we're going to set it to zero stone, zero pounds, and zero ounces. Spoons can't possibly lose."

CHAPTER TWELVE

In which Lady Llewella remembers each minor miscalculation, but forgets her age.

"WHATEVER you win GAMBLING, you'll always lose your soul."

Teddy considered this nuanced sentiment, along with a two-tone drawing of Satan before a flaming tote board offering appalling odds, from a pamphlet provided by Aunty Azalea as essential cover.

"You sure you can spare it?" she asked. "This crowd must positively clamour for them."

"Everybody gives me a very wide berth," reported Azalea happily. "When they do look at me, it's as though I'm invisible. It's been just lovely."

"I'm glad for you, Aunty, but don't forget you're not just here to enjoy the nice weather and ostracism," Teddy reminded her. "We also need a complete and detailed census of all the short bearded chaps who pass, with particular attention given to those whose beards are clearly horse hair."

Teddy and Azalea were positioned near the entrance of the tea tent, which, with the beer garden, formed the gateway to the alley of produce and promotions that led to the entrance to Bromford Bridge Racecourse Park. The punting public would have their passports metaphorically stamped by Azalea's concentrated diffidence, even if most of them hadn't been slowed to a brief stop by the beer garden.

"Gentlemen don't seem to be going in very much for full beards these days, and those that do tend to be quite tall," observed Azalea. "I think your short men are somehow attaching their beards after entering the park."

Teddy surveyed the intermission crowd. "I thought of that. Oy Roy and Chard the leg man are on notice track-side. Why, have you seen a lot of short beardless chaps?"

"None at all."

"What about little old grey haired ladies? Seen any of those, present company excluded?"

"Just the tea ladies."

"Yes…" Teddy steadied a suspicious squint on the six ladies waiting behind their tables of tea and cakes. "Have any of the tea ladies left their station at any time?"

"Oh, no." Azalea raised two scandalised eyebrows on behalf of the unstained reputation of the Middleditch tea ladies. "No, they would never leave their stations unattended."

"Right…" Teddy considered this with a nodding realisation. "Any punters coming and lingering over the scones for longer than one ought normally need to decide whether or not to have a scone?"

"Oddly enough…" Azalea spoke with rising recollection. "There've been almost no customers at all."

In that moment the patently obvious elected to demonstrate itself in the form of two sunny sportsmen, flush with fresh winnings and eager to spend some of it on tea and scones. They rolled happily and hungrily up to the tea tent and, for a moment, smiled at Teddy and Azalea, until their eyes fell upon the heavy cross and heavier literature, and their smiles soon followed. They stopped where they were, as though having stepped into a rabbit warren.

"Oh, uh, what ho, Tom," said the one to the other, "why, looky there, there's a choir."

Then the two chaps doffed their bowlers and went to the beer garden.

'Oh dear." Azalea squinted quizzically at the evading crowd. "Am I the reason no one's going into the tea tent?"

'We'll make it up to them," said Teddy. "I'll send Uncle Markham here for his victory tea."

Azalea assumed a pained expression, much like that which she shows her butler, Puckeridge, when he tells her that someone is on the telephone.

"I don't think you ought to do that, Teddy."

"Too downmarket, you think? Don't worry about Uncle Markham — he's wearing Wellington boots and a cloth cap with swallowtails, and his waistcoat is inside out."

Whatever it was that so vexed Azalea, it had reached and

passed a very specific threshold, and she could no longer verbalise it. She simply shook her head, quickly and within a tight range, as though hoping the action might be confused with a lady-like shiver.

Her suspicions duly raised, Teddy craned around the shivering aunty for a proper squint at the dark recesses of the tea tent. There, sitting side-by-side and sharing a buttered crumpet and what looked a cheeky titter, were Lady Llewella Middleditch and Vicar Bittles.

❦

"More tea? Or should I just send the violinist over, and leave you two alone"

Teddy proposed this range of options with the light touch of a blacksmith on a deadline.

Vicar Bittles cocked his hinterland handsome head in a fashion that would have been found innocent on all charges, but Lady Lew reflexively catapulted a teaspoon of sugar into the air, from whence it rained down onto her bird's nest fascinator.

"I say, Vicar, that is a bang up choir." Teddy took the liberty of the facing chair. "It's one thing to knock out your textbook hymns, but I don't know that I've ever heard such a spirited rendition of *Keyhole in the Door.*"

"The boys are singing sea shanties?" Vicar Bittles smiled with a bemused, tireless patience.

"Not exclusively, no," reported Teddy. "They just finished a call-and-response version of *Stockings on the Floor,* and I think that's more of a ballad, isn't it?"

"I must go, Your Ladyship." On his way out of the tent, Vicar Bittles thanked each of the tea ladies individually.

"Call me Lew..." mewed Lady Llewella, adding, should the proposal prove too familiar, "Ha ha."

"Is he married, Aunty Lew?" Teddy tipped the vicar's tea onto the grass beneath the table and poured herself a fresh cup of the tepid dirty water that is the most beloved of the cherished fare of the English travelling tea tent.

"No..." Lady Lew replied with learned suspicion.

"Oh, well, that's all right then, isn't it?" Teddy sat back with

101

her cup and regarded her aunt. "Only one party needs to be unmarried in these cases, I think."

"I don't know to which cases you could possibly refer."

"The cases of middle-aged ladies making fools of themselves." Teddy checked the inevitable objections with a raised hand, and sipped her grey runoff. "I saw you. You looked like you'd just met Rudolph Valentino on a school outing."

"Mister Bittles?" Lady Lew laughed a rippling laugh, as hollow as a hull. "We just get along so well, Teddy. He's ever clever, don't you know... and quite keen on horses... and we both appreciate the poetry of Blake and Gerard Stanley Hopkins."

"Manley Hopkins."

Lady Lew's mask of nervous bonhomie fell away. "And he's not always correcting me," she raised a proud chin, spilling sugar from her fascinator down her back, "and he's not always trying to auction off my horse."

"Uncle Markham isn't trying to auction off Spoons." Teddy, familiar with the flavour of the infinite-use tea leaf, tried swirling the pot. "He's just dotty."

"Well he shouldn't be."

"My recollections of the occasion are a bit foggy, what with it taking place before I was born, but are you intimating that Lord Markham Middleditch wasn't dotty when you married him?"

"It accumulates, Teddy." Lady Middleditch stirred her cup of mostly milk with the stiff swirls of wounded pride. "This year he installed an aviary, of all things, on the plateau, overlooking the home stretch."

"I didn't see any aviary."

"The foundation caused a mudslide. It's in the east garden, now, where my Uffington White Horse, depicted in white vinca, used to be." Lady Lew gazed poutily into her watery milk, wherein was reflected drowned periwinkle. "And I can't replant, because now the east garden is under two feet of sediment belted in by a forsythia hedge and a bulwark made of sandbags and my gardening barrow, which is the only thing preventing the south end of the trench filling with mud."

'Well, what of it?" asked Teddy. "It's not as though Uncle Mark flooded your garden deliberately. In an adult, healthy marriage a mature woman would just fill his nightshirt with horse hair clippings and move right on, all while maintaining a respectable, vicar-ladyship relationship with Mister Bittles."

"And the vicar, unlike Markham, doesn't pursue an inexhaustible series of mad measures to get horses to run faster." Lady Lew settled her gaze meaningfully on the grassy concourse, where Vicar Bittles was helping a little boy rescue a butterfly from a puddle. "Inspirational stories, chickens, Irish reels — did you see the ceiling of the stable?"

"Recently?" asked Teddy. "Or ever? In either case, no."

"It's painted."

"Is that unusual?"

"It's painted just like the Sistine Chapel, except Adam is Flying Fox, winner of the Triple Crown in 1899."

"Do the horses like it?"

"Horses can't look up, Teddy. Markham remembered that after he'd commissioned the work, which explains the mural in the fashion of the Bayeux Tapestry."

"I really have to see this stable."

"And now all these absurd experiments are going to get us warned off every racecourse in the country."

"And France, probably," addendumed Teddy, helpfully.

Lady Lew lowered and tightened her voice into the sort of hiss that snakes employ when they gossip. "All the while, Lord Bitterbrook is enjoying the best room in the castle, getting himself around four frankly astonishingly large meals a day, and borrowing everything that he can fit in a trunk, plus a trunk."

"I thought it was you who invited them."

"Of course, one is civil to one's old friends from school," sniffed Lady Lew.

"Until they start to hog all the vicars."

"Who changes for tea, in this day and age?" exasperated Lew, trying and very nearly striking a frequency between scandalised and narcoleptically indifferent. "She has an outfit for backgammon. So of course she needs an entire second room for her wardrobe."

"She has a what now?"

"Madness, I know. And it's *just* for backgammon — she has a completely different ensemble for whist."

"No, did you say that Lady Olivia has a second room?"

In that moment the attention of Teddy and Lew was drawn to the green just beyond the open walls of the tea tent by a sort of 'eep' sound, not unlike the alarm call of the common house sparrow when called by name by a magistrate. They looked to see Aunty Azalea, holding up temperance pamphlets to Lord Bitterbrook like Van Helsing showing a cross to Dracula.

Bitterbrook received the literature with a confused grace and then, spotting Teddy and Lady Lew, backed carefully away from Aunty Azalea and wandered into the tea tent. He issued a stiff nod of contrived surprise and then affected to be distracted by the misshapen scones and lopsided seed cake.

He stood by his standard selection of two of everything and tea, relied on recognition to cover it all on Lord Markham's cuff (having left all his money with Lady Bitterbrook, sadly), and lowered the plate of pastries and pot of puddle onto Teddy's table with a sigh of relief that spoke of uncountable hours on unaccustomed feet.

"What ho, Sticky," greeted Teddy. "Having a good card? You must have enjoyed the sixth race, when Solitary Salmon threw her jockey. It looked for a bit that he might have been seriously injured — you must have laughed yourself silly."

Lady Llewella, sensing that this remark might be open to interpretation, covered neatly with, "Ah hahahahahaha," and overpoured her teacup.

"I didn't know you were interested in that sort of thing, Lord Sticky." Teddy tapped the top of two temperance pamphlets, titled, 'Signed in Whisky and Sin: Seal Your Deal With Satan.'

Bitterbrook, a cup of milky water in one hand and a crumbly scone in the other, glanced at the blurry title. As it happens, he had approached Aunty Azalea because he had heard about a silver-haired track tout who never failed to predict a winner. Accordingly, he approached the only silver-haired old lady he'd seen all day and asked her, from behind a discreet hand, "What do you think of Shenanigan in the final?"

Azalea had responded as instructed — she held up her pamphlets as a deterrent and closed her eyes. In that moment, Lord Bitterbrook spotted Teddy and Lady Llewella and so he casually and conspiratorially took receipt of the pamphlets and withdrew, convinced more than ever that Azalea was an ingeniously disguised track tout, and unwilling to share the secret.

And so when Teddy said she didn't know that he was interested in that sort of thing, he replied quickly and cleverly, "Oh, yes, very much so." Then, storing an entire scone in his mouth, he withdrew his pince-nez (or, more accurately, the pince-nez he'd taken with him that morning) and put them on his nose.

Teddy took note that the specs were of a fashionable, feminine design, with damascene frames and matching chatelaine joined by a fine filament chain. Teddy therefore said, "You have surprisingly progressive views, Lord Sticky."

"Eh?" Sticky stared hard from behind the impenetrable prescription of Lady Brimble. "Oh, well, one must keep up with the times."

"You agree with the general sentiment of these pamphlets, do you?"

"Uhm, yes, in a general principle sort of way," shammed Sticky. "Naturally one takes issue with certain practicalities…"

"But in general you would agree that…" Teddy took up the 'Seal the Deal' tract, from which she feigned to quote; "…the proletariat will not be free 'fore every noble swings from a tree."

Lord Bitterbrook considered admitting that he couldn't read through spectacles that were not his. He chewed on this prospect and a scone for a moment, before realising how foolhardy that would be. He cleared his pallet with a cup of cold milkwater, put Lady Brimble's pince-nez in his pocket, and said, with the confidence of his convictions, "I remain open to all manner of opinion, Teddy. I'm a peer of the realm, a member of the House of Lords. For a man in my position it's vitally important that I keep myself informed of all that goes on around me."

"Ha hahaha ha," agreed Lady Llewella.

CHAPTER THIRTEEN

In which a punter has a fancy and Stilts discovers his hidden powers of persuasion.

"FOR A MAN IN MY POSITION it's vitally important that I keep myself informed of all that goes on around me."

In the beer garden, after the eighth and final race, Oy Roy was expressing almost word-for-word the sentiments of Lord Bitterbrook, except that what he actually said was, "A man of my bold and honest, it's all blarney and botheration, innit, if I ain't got the straight griffin."

As today was a working day, Oy wore his working clothes. His crimson cap would have matched his crimson coat, had it been a little brighter, and had the coat not slight yellow stripes no wider than Oy's thumb. The stripes had the additional feature of irregular widths and frequencies and, on the pockets, they were horizontal. Oy wore a green cravat ornamented with golden horseshoes and his green trousers were tucked into his race-day boots, which had wooden heels and soles, rendering the bookie six inches taller and all but crippled.

Oy stood at a barrel which served as a table, thus distinguishing the beer garden from a beer terrace or a space outside where people are drinking beer. Teddy was with him, nodding sympathetically, and they were both waiting for Stilts to wade through the post-race masses with three pints of warm stale ale.

"Don't it just tot *(doesn't it figure),* half me hedges on Loosey Lacey in the lemon *(I invested half my insurance on Loosey Lacey to win the third race)* and don't she just bag the post by a short head *(she won)* but then she's straight pattered out *(she was disqualified)."*

"Gruelling ruling, that." Stilts swung the pints home. "Her rider weighed in at half a pound less than he weighed out before the race — you'd think they'd let it pass, a young outsider like Lacey. She must be heartbroken."

"I'll tell you what it is, just a conspiracy, is all." Oy drew deeply from his pint, and returned it to the barrel like a gavel. "Another day like this and I'll be ruined."

Meanwhile, Chard the leg man was standing outside the beer garden, squinting in and trying to distinguish Oy Roy's branded ensemble from the orange and purple plaid, pink paisley, and multi-coloured patchwork of the competition. In the end, he spotted Stilts, and pushed urgently through the crowd.

"'Allo Miss, Mister Roy, Mister Stilts." Chard quickly scanned the crowd of competitors for eavesdroppers, and then beckoned Stilts to lower his ear into the zone of confidentiality. "Can you from your vantage point, Mister Stilts, make out a bloke in a cloth cap and a smile on his dial what looks like he just won a hundred quid?"

Stilts craned up and surveyed the distant terrain. He returned with his report; "Yes."

"He just won a hundred quid."

"Is that unusual?" wondered Teddy. "I myself am up half a shilling on the day."

"It's unusual for this bloke, who to my reading is the stamp what normally chooses his horses by the colour of the jockey's silks and dares no more than a pound a punt, but I find him this morning or, to put it more as it was, he finds me, and tells me to put my shirt on Shropshire Lass in the first."

"Three lengths at 12-to-1," recalled Stilts. "I very nearly bet on her, too, but then I didn't."

"Well he didn't nearly bet on her, he laid down his little all — eight quid."

"Daring," toasted Teddy.

"He had a fancy, so he said," recounted Chard. "But then, when he comes to collect, he confesses that it weren't no fancy, but it was a sweet old nan what give him the tip."

Everyone turned now to look at the man with the cloth cap and fancy, but only Stilts could see him.

"Stilts, go and be charming," instructed Teddy. "Discuss sports and... what is it blokes talk about? Hats? Talk about hats."

"Charming, Teddy? Me?"

"Imagine he's my father, and you're asking for my hand in marriage."

"You said your father doesn't like me."

"He doesn't. Not at all," confirmed Teddy. "And this chap doesn't even know you, so you're already odds-on. You need to get him to introduce you to his nan tout."

"Oh, right oh."

"And take him to the tea tent. Get him to take a good look at the tea ladies."

"Oh, uhm, right oh."

"They're the only little old ladies on site — it's got to be one of them."

Collin's smile held and probably would for several weeks, but he'd have been happier still had he been able to squeeze into the beer garden and order himself a well-earned victory pint. It fell well that he'd had such an historic win, but it would have been better yet had it fallen later in the day. He'd won a hundred pounds on the first of eight races, and so Collin had passed the entire remainder of the day hoarding his winnings.

Now, though, was the moment to indulge himself, to order the finest ale the beer garden offered and perhaps be drawn into conversation with one of the younger novice punters who might benefit from hearing his veteran account of a day well won. Mostly, though, Collin wanted a pint of beer.

"Have a good card?"

Collin turned on the friendly hail and saw a waistcoat. Wavering above this trim black waistcoat and chestnut herringbone tailoring wizardry was a broad smile fitted with difficulty onto a thin face.

"Quite satisfactory, yes," offhanded Collin. "You?"

"Oh, rather," enthused Stilts, without wasting so much as a moment on thought. "Twenty quid on the favourite in the fourth because he's a personal friend, a very profitable little winner and placer in the sixth because I couldn't decide so I flipped a coin and lost it in a ditch, and a blunt shunt punt on Saffron Sun in the sixth, who came home carrying 5-to-1 and a very startled jockey."

Stilts ended his sporting bulletin with a beaming smile which, he was initially surprised to find, was not returned.

"Oh, right." Collin resumed examining the crowd for cracks. "Well done."

Stilts, finally, remembered that he was meant to be charming and, with further reflection, that not everyone is charmed by other's tales of trackside success.

"Lost it all on the eighth, mind," claimed Stilts. "Spread it all out on six each-ways."

"Ah, well, that's where you went wrong, if you don't mind my saying so." Collin, visibly cheered, removed his cap and met Stilts' innocent gaze with the wry eye of the seasoned handicapper. "I pick my horse very careful. I study the field, the grounds, the weather — mustn't overlook the weather — and note that I said horse and not horses — I never bet on more than one in a race."

"Not really."

"Point of fact, I only placed the one bet all day," revealed Collin. "Sometimes that's how the field develops, I like to say."

"Tilden." Stilts, behind a stiff smile, knew that he had his work cut out for him. "Friends call me Stilts."

"Collin."

"Come and have a drink, Collin."

"I will, thanks." Collin shifted sideways, such as to better fit into the beer garden throng.

"Not there." Stilts turned to indicate the calm Shangri-la that was the tea tent.

"I think I'd prefer a pint," said Collin in full and frank admission.

"That's because you haven't had the tea made by the Middleditch tea ladies." Stilts moved towards the tea tent. "It's famous all over Shropshire."

"Nevertheless..."

"There's something you need to see in the tea tent," blurted Stilts

"Oh yes? What's that then?"

"The tea ladies." In the absence of a gift for instantaneous invention, Stilts told the truth, and hoped it would somehow evolve into something clever.

"You want me to see the tea ladies?"

"They're lovely." Stilts danced anxiously from foot to foot. "I mean, their scones. Their scones are lovely."

Stilts lured and led Collin, like a nesting tern feigning a broken wing to draw a fox away from her young. Collin wanted a beer, but he also wanted an audience, and at the moment Stilts was the bird in the hand. He followed lopingly to the tea tent, but glanced longingly back at the beer garden.

Aunty Azalea, happily, was not at her post, because a temperance campaigner would certainly have decided Collin solidly in favour of beer. As it was, he went in and took a table in the otherwise empty tea tent while Stilts secured a pot of this famous tea and a plate of these picturesque scones.

Stilts returned. Despite choosing carefully, he placed a plate of what looked like naturally-occuring mineral deposits on the table, alongside a pot of cooling kettle water. He poured Collin and then himself generous cups.

Collin regarded with undisguised disappointment his cup of clear water.

"It's meant to be like that," Stilts assured him. "Once they find a tea ball that does the trick, they like to stick with it."

Pre-empting further evaluation, Stilts added six spoons of sugar to Collin's cup.

"So you only bet on a single horse..." Stilts emptied the creamer into Collin's tea, which took on a disturbingly wan tone, like slush. "How, ehm, how did you select your horse?"

Collin gazed thirstily at the laughing, drinking crowd in the beer tent, and sipped his tea.

"It's cold."

"Yes," enthused Stilts, "and quite reasonably priced, too. You were saying how you chose your bet."

'As I say, I consider all the angles..." Unconsciously, Collin blew on his tea. "Now you take the first race — it was a broad field, and Shropshire Lass was far from the favourite. There was also, ehm..."

'Knotty Scotty, two-year-old stallion, was odds-on at 1-to-1."

"Knotty Scotty, for instance, was definitely worth considering, but I rarely like the favourite, me."

"No."

"No. I like to play the odds. And then there's the qualifications — now the first race was a maiden race for two-year-olds..."

"Handicap for any age carrying up to a stone, all maidens favoured two pounds, I think you mean."

"That's right. I mean handicap for... for what you said."

Stilts, in a measure that he hoped would freeze time while he regrouped and refined his strategy, drew deeply on his tea and then smiled as a bulwark against the instant impulse to spit it on the ground.

A burst of laughter from the beer tent drew a yearning gaze from Collin.

"Have a scone," Stilts almost sang. "They work so hard on their scones." Stilts turned and waved at the tea ladies. "They do like a little wave, Collin."

Collin smiled weakly and waved vaguely.

"I mean to say, specifically, give that one by the door a wave. Doris, I think her name is."

Collin waved at the tea lady whose name was, in fact, Betty.

"You've never seen her before, have you Collin?"

"The tea lady? No, I don't think so."

"What about the next one? With the seed cakes." Stilts, as a reminder, was not a gifted extemporaneous speaker. "Dora is her name, I believe."

Collin, with considerably less enthusiasm, smiled and waved at Lotti, the seed cake tea lady. And so on like that through all six tea ladies, until Stilts was confident that Collin was either a master actor or had never seen any of these ladies before.

And so, with a sad, internal and eternal resignation, Stilts fell back on the one gift on which he always seemed to be falling back.

"Tell me your source, Collin, and I'll reach right over the heads of that lot in the beer garden and get you a pint of ale, and keep them coming until they bar us."

Without hesitation, Collin replied, "A sweet little old lady. Sidled up to me at the choir and told me, Shropshire Lass in the first, sure as anything."

"And you believed her?"

"The choir was singing the Hallelujah Chorus."

"Oh, right." Stilts nodded reverentially. "Literally a sign from God."

"Just so. At any rate, it certainly paid out."

"And this sweet little grey-haired old lady didn't ask you for any sort of consideration?" wondered Stilts. "Just gave you Shropshire Lass and then vanished on the wind?"

"Just like that." Collin spoke with wide-eyed earnestness. "But then she found me later, just after I collected, and said that for a fair share of my winnings, she'd give me another tip for nothing."

"Oh, really?" Stilts, by instinct, now endeavoured — and failed — to appear disinterested. "And, uhm, did she?"

"She did," said Collin, with awe in his voice, as though he dare not believe it himself. "A claim race, right here on Monday, is going to be won by a horse named Spoons."

CHAPTER FOURTEEN

In which Teddy sets a scene, Stilts sets a record, and Spoons and Chicken set aside their differences.

"SO, THAT BIT'S ALL RIGHT THEN — Spoons is going to win his claim race."

Stilts raised the issue again after dinner during a spontaneously arranged walk with Teddy to view the slurry sea that was the east garden, and to speculate in confidence.

"And we know that because Collin, a novice punter if ever there was one, bought the tip from an unidentified and, by all accounts, unidentifiable sweet little old grey-haired archetype," reiterated Teddy.

"Just so. Solid as sunrise."

Teddy and Stilts followed a path which traced the top edge of the trench and was composed of floor tiles, surplus from a turn-of-the-last-century kitchen renovation. Teddy was outfitted for the weather and wet ground in wellies and a fisherman's slicker with hood, and Stilts wore his riding boots and plaid cape and deerstalker, giving him something of the aspect of a birch tree understudying Sherlock Holmes.

"Assuming that her information is good, we still don't know who she is nor how she knows." Teddy stopped and surveyed the windows of the first floor of the castle, which were more or less at the same altitude as the top of the trench. The evening was dark and damp at some blurry border between light rain and heavy fog. Warm yellow lights flickered in the windows of the library and games room, and Teddy could make out the silhouette of Lady Llewella, laughing nervously. "Who's telling sweet little old ladies which horses are going to win, and why, and how does he or she or they know which horses are going to win? Where are you going, Stilts?"

Stilts was not so much going somewhere as standing right where he was as where he was slid slowly downhill towards the ground floor of the castle.

"Ehm, that way, roughly." Stilts pointed with the peak of his cap. "Not sure I have much say in the matter. Join me?"

As it happened, the path split at Stilts' departure point, branching into a rough stairway formed of broken crockery and flower pots.

"In fact, I have business at the bottom of the trench." Teddy took to the stairs in time with Stilts' erratic but easily matched pace. "And what if whoever is tipping off the little old ladies is the same party giving winners to Jimmy Fairly's short bearded hustler?"

"A not entirely improbable proposition," said Stilts as he ducked to avoid a branch. "In fact, Jimmy says it's a conspiracy. He tells me that the bearded chappy put fifty quid on Chockit Rockit "

Stilts sped away at this point, as the incline had steepened, and he struggled to maintain his balance in a frantic dance that put Teddy in mind of a newly born foal.

Teddy joined him at the bottom of the trench, where Stilts had come to a stop in the branches of a small conifer.

"Fairly's pint of punter was there today? How did we fail to see him? We had spies everywhere at the entrance and trackside."

"The stables?"

Teddy continued into the shadowy ravine between the east wall and the muddy grade. She stopped by a window, under which lay a grainstore block and tackle. One end of its rope led up and into a dark window, and the other lay in a coil in the yard.

"Well, exactly — the stables. Neither Shortbeard nor Sweet Little Old Lady passed the entrance, and yet they were both on hand with inside information." Teddy handed Stilts a rope end. "Take ahold of that."

"Right oh."

"Leaving us with the question, Stilters, who can we trust?"

"Me."

"Yes, that's true, and of tremendous comfort." Teddy tested the action of the pulleys. "Just run that end up the hill, will you?"

Stilts looked up into the shimmering ascent, glistening in the hazy moonlight. "That great higher of mire, Teddy? It's unscalable."

"It's barely twenty feet."

"Of thick slick," pointed out Stilts. "I'll bet that's what happened to George Mallory."

"You want me to do it?"

"Oh..." Stilts took up a felled twig to serve as a walking stick, "...right oh."

Stilts methodically tried and failed several approaches, from the side-by-side technique favoured by Alpine skiers to Charlie Chaplin's patented herringbone pattern, before stepping back and taking a running start that put him half-way up the hill, holding onto a sapling. This unexpected success left him stranded, and with time to reflect.

"You trust Lord Markham, though, don't you?"

"Do I?" returned Teddy. "The man seems strangely determined to incriminate himself. Rather puts me in mind of Mapps Manning — fellow member of the Ladies' Auto Club, four and half litre Bentley for city driving and a gold-finished Bugatti 35C for country."

"Ehm."

"Had a record win in last year's Newport to Norwich via Northampton rally, but then immediately grassed herself up for getting help changing a tire outside Swindon and taking a detour to Kettering to help out a vicar whose bicycle had been nicked."

"Very honourable." Stilts skied slowly backwards and unintentionally down the hill. "It's only winning if it's done by the rules."

"This was the view of the stewards," agreed Teddy, "and so the transgressions were overlooked, and they appeared to explain why no one saw her on the road between Northamptom and Norwich, though it may also have been related to the fact that she took a train from Kettering to Beccles, where she kept a second gold-finish Bugatti 35C."

"You think Lord Markham has a second Chockit Rockit?" Stilts took another run at the hill, high-stepping like a hurdler doing the Can-Can, and managed to establish a new base camp on a little plateau formed by a dense community of refugee periwinkles.

"That would explain a lot, but a ringer is unlikely in the case of a horse that changes colour with its mood."

"Pox, I've lost my stick." Stilts surveyed the muddy grade

which was, in fact, littered with twigs, many of which bore remarkable similarity to his. "What about Lady Llewella? You must trust her."

'I have private cause to believe that Aunty Lulu is inconstant, Stilts, and unsound on the poetry of Gerard Manley Hopkins," said Teddy with cool decision. "Why don't you just step up the rest of the way?"

Stilts levelled a squinting appraisal on the remaining distance from base camp to the summit and recalled that he was, in fact, quite tall.

'Oh, right." Stilts stepped easily up to where the east garden used to be at the top of Middleditch Castle Ditch. "What about Lady Olivia? She's a lady in her own right, you know — her father is Lord Beccles."

"What does that prove? My uncle is Lord Middleditch and I have a second cousin once removed who's Master of the Horse, and I'm wanted by the London police under two names." Teddy played a yard of rope out of the block and tackle. "Tie that to something, will you, Stilts? In any case, it's as clear as clean crystal that whatever it is that Lord Bitterbrook is up to, he's not the mastermind."

Stilts weaved the rope through branches and barrow and knotted it with a quick half-windsor.

"I say, Tedds — purely out of curiosity, why am I tying a rope to the top of the hill?"

"I should have thought that would have been obvious, Stilts — it's so you can climb down safely."

"Oh, right. Handy, that." Stilts set about with the best of intentions to climb down safely, hand over hand on the rope, lost his rhythm and his grip, and skated downhill with the precise grace and legerdemain of fledgling bagpipes leaving the nest. He glided to a stop and he and Teddy shared a moment of silent awe that he was still on his feet.

"What about Mister Yardpole?" asked Stilts. "Surely we can trust Mister Yardpole."

'The man is the purest of hug-bunnies, but I wouldn't trust him to keep a secret if he were chained to it at the wrist."

'Marshpool?"

'In matters of love and discretion the man has the worst

judgement of anyone I know, present company excepted, of course."

"Oy Roy?"

"A bookmaker with a heart of gold?" marvelled Teddy. "I suppose it's possible, but the odds are very long indeed."

"Jimmy Fairly, then," proposed Stilts. "He's a spiffing chap, but almost completely heartless."

"I never trust anyone with more than one alias and less than three, I think you know that, Stilts."

As this series of verdicts was being weighed, Teddy and Stilts descended further into the darkness of the east valley, until they came to a broad double door which, two hundred years and four yards of sinkage ago, had been a morning terrace. They entered here the ground floor of Middleditch Castle which, functionally, was the dim downstairs. They passed through the mudroom, where they cleaned their boots, and then the second mudroom, where they took off their boots, and then into the corridor, where they encountered Marshpool, who was lighting a cigarette from the embers of another cigarette.

"What ho, Marshpool," greeted Teddy as she emerged from the shadows.

"Gah!" replied the butler, simultaneously burning his fingers and upper lip. "I was... just... looking for... a thing."

"It's me, Marshington."

"Oh, hello Miss, evening Mister Stollery." Marshpool brushed smouldering cinders from his morning coat and spoke in the hush of the undercover asset. "All clear."

"Excellent work, Mishmarsh, and you're barely even on fire," lauded Teddy. "Just one final thing, if you can fit it in between overseeing cocktails in the library and worrying – will you please ask Lady Middleditch and Lady Bitterbrook to join me in the games room for a nightcap sherry at ten o'clock."

Marshpool added the mental note to a disordered stack of mental notes, and watched Teddy and Stilts pad in stocking feet to and up the stairs. Then he assumed the wary squint of the canny dodger, and slipped noiselessly out and into the darkness. Unknowingly retracing the steps of Teddy and Stilts, the butler was soon at the northern tip of the trench, observing the residents through the windows of the library and games room. He withdrew his pocket watch and determined after careful study that he couldn't read it in the darkness, and then slipped and skidded to the stables.

The stables were warm and sultry in that weighty way common to low buildings full of large animals. It was mainly silent, too, but for the occasional snort of a horse recalling something amusing or issuing an ultimatum to a fly. Marshpool shuffled through the straw, wishing for a cigarette or a torch or a chance to go back in time and answer differently to the choices that led him to be pressured into spying on horses at night.

Nonetheless, he proceeded. He crouched, for some reason, between stalls, rising just enough to peer over the top of each door until he spotted his target, and his target spotted him.

Spoons was pleased to see Marshpool, although he didn't entirely know why. In his simple, thoroughbred way, he saw a kinship in the eyes of the skittish butler, but in the main Spoons would have welcomed with equal delight a visit from Woolly Man or Sing-Songy Bloke or Cloth Cap Chap who is, in fact, two different stable lads. Anyone at all would have been an improvement because it would have been a change from the current ambient gloom which had lingered now, to the best of Spoons' recollection, since the beginning of time — Chicken had deserted him. The details were, putting it charitably, foggy, but the essential facts were that Chicken had been there and now wasn't, and Spoons was quite sure that he preferred it when Chicken was there.

So Spoons blinked hopeful, mopeful eyes at the top of half of Marshpool's head, and he twitched an optimistic ear. Marshpool, however, having completed his reconnaissance, slowly descended out of view, and Spoons instantly forgot that he'd ever been there.

Emboldened by success, Marshpool moved like a fox from stall to stall back towards the door. The instant he placed his hand on the latch, however, it bucked like a thing alive, and the door began to open.

Markham Lord Middleditch, dressed for a damp evening in a worn cardigan over a velvet cummerbund above mucking trousers and wellies, stole into the stable and closed the door behind him in what he believed to be — but was most manifestly not — a discreet manner. As his eyes adjusted to the darkness, he thought he detected a figure scurrying fox-like into the shadows beyond. Lord Markham, as a precaution, pulled his cap slightly lower on his head, hiked his package under his arm, and skulked down the corridor, zig-zagging such that he might whisper compliments of the evening to each and every horse.

Finally, Lord Markham stopped at the last stall on the left, balanced his case on a saddlerack, opened it, and withdrew an apple, which he passed over the gate to Chockit Rockit, who received it gratefully. Then His Lordship took out his violin and put it to his chin. He plucked the strings discerningly, lay his bow across them, and gazed with an artist's soul out the window of Chockit Rockit's stall at the gradient grey diffusion of moonlight on fog. Then he began to play.

With all this talk of whether or not Lord Markham could or should or would influence the performance of a horse by playing certain selections on the violin, it would have been helpful to know, probably, that he is the worst violin player for hundreds of miles in any direction, and that includes many who have given up the instrument and even several who've never tried it.

Chockit Rockit was indifferent. He didn't know that Lord Markham was playing *Dunmore Lasses* nor, for that matter, an Irish reel nor, for yet that matter, the violin. Chockit Rockit associated the screechy din with apples and Lord Markham, both of whom he liked, and with running around the course with his mates, which he liked even more. Accordingly, he pawed reflexively at the floor of his stall, a movement which Lord Markham took as keeping time with the music. However, Marshpool, who, it can now be revealed, was hiding in Chockit Rockit's stall, received the action as something more in the nature of an imminent peril. He stood up.

"Marshpool?" With a short, scratchy A#, Lord Markham ceased doing what he'd been doing to the violin.

"Good evening, Your Lordship." Marshpool leaned casually

on the stall gate, thought the better of it, and instead stood on one foot. 'Lovely evening."

"Marshpool, what are you doing in the stable?"

"I was looking... for..." Marshpool instinctively threw out his standard line of defense without knowing what was at the other end. "...you, sir. I was looking for you."

"In Chockit Rockit's stall?"

"Hm?"

"You were looking for me in Chockit Rockit's stall?"

"Oh, no, Your Lordship," insisted Marshpool, with a decisive wave. "I didn't know it was his stall."

"Oh, I see."

"Quite so."

"Why were you looking for me, Marshpool?"

The butler blinked at the viscount in the darkness and, unconsciously, nodded his head in thought. The horse pluttered impatiently.

"Miss Quillfeather!" Marshpool nearly shouted but, to his credit, resisted snapping his fingers. "Miss Quilleather asked me to extend an invitation to Her Ladyship and Her Ladyship for sherry in the games room."

"Ah, yes. I see," alleged Lord Markham. "Oh, ehm, Marshpool, would it not have been simpler to put the proposal directly to Lady Llewella?"

Marshpool put a meditative hand to his chin. "Put the proposal directly to Her Ladyship. Yes, yes I see what you mean, sir. Would you in future prefer that I do so, Your Lordship?"

"Only if you think it best," said Lord Markham. "I've never had much talent for decorum."

'Every great house is different, in my experience, My Lord. In my previous situation, at Handsome Hall, such occasions were always announced with a live cannon."

'Ah, no, that would never do here, Marshpool," said Lord Markham with uncharacteristic decision. "It would upset the horses."

'Just as you wish, sir."

Lord Markham puzzled with a sort of complacent awe at the immeasurable vastness of the conventions of English country life as he returned to the castle, and so he was caught off guard as he climbed the main stairs and encountered Lady Bitterbrook coming down.

"Good evening, Markham. Have you been playing your violin?"

Markham, keenly and constantly aware of Teddy's warning to tell no one about his secret method for encouraging Chockit Rockit to remarkable turns of speed, briefly considered claiming that he didn't play the violin. After a moment's reflection he realised that the claim lacked credibility, because he was carrying a violin.

"Yes." Markham smiled at his ready guile, but something in Lady Olivia's aspect suggested that she expected more. "I was playing for Marshpool."

"You were playing your violin for the butler."

"Precisely," said Markham, as though applauding her snap comprehension. "Speaking of whom, he would like to invite you for a nightcap sherry in the games room."

"Marshpool wishes to invite me for a nightcap?"

"He would ask you himself," confided Lord Markham, "but it would upset the horses."

"May I take it, Markham, that Marshpool has been asked by Lady Llewella to serve evening sherry in the games room?"

"Ah, no, Teddy. My niece Teddy is arranging drinks in the games room," corrected Lord Markham, "But Llewella is invited, too."

"Llewella is organising a nightcap sherry in the library," reported Lady Olivia to Lord Bitterbrook when she'd returned to their room. "What do you suppose it means?"

"Must it mean anything at all?" wondered Sticky, who was wearing Lord Markham's pince-nez and reading *The Times*.

"It may at the very least present an opportunity." Lady Olivia went into her room, such that the ensuing conversation was held at high volume. "Markham is clearly up to something."

"What makes you say that?"

"He had his violin with him," Olivia said from within her cocktail gown wardrobe. "I must speak very sternly to Alice — positively everything has been hung mismatched."

"He was probably playing his violin for his horses," soothed Sticky. "He thinks it makes them run faster."

"I need to go to my wardrobe room." Olivia returned to the salon suite and seized the bell pull. "Perhaps Markham's violin does make his horses run faster — clearly something was brought to bear on Chockit Rockit at Cheveley."

"All the better," Lord Bitterbrook called it.

"I think not, Stanley," differed Her Ladyship coolly. "We'll never get hold of Chockit Rockit, now, at any price, and Monday's claim race may well be our best and only chance to acquire Spoons, unless Markham has some way of guaranteeing that he'll win."

"I'm quite confident that he *will* win."

Lady Olivia levelled a suspicious squint on her husband. "You're oddly resigned to the prospect. Need I remind you that if Spoons wins then he'll go to auction, and Markham can double anything you can bid."

"If he doesn't win, then he goes to claim," Sticky reminded her. "Which means that his new owner will be selected by lot, but if he wins, then he'll go to auction, and Lord Markham won't ever bid."

"Why would Markham not bid on Spoons?"

"I'm going to tell him that if he does, I shall inform the stewards that he bet on Chockit Rockit to win Cheveley, and then he'll be warned off for life."

"Did he bet on Chockit Rockit to win Cheveley?" hoped Olivia.

"His shirt, apparently," confirmed Sticky. "So now all that remains is for Spoons to win handily on Monday."

CHAPTER FIFTEEN

Featuring double dealings, double meanings, double cousins, double crosses, and double doses of double gin-and-tonics.

"NOW ALL THAT REMAINS is for Spoons to win handily on Monday."

Lord Markham mirrored this simple expedient to Lady Lulu while searching his writing desk for his pince-nez and copy of *The Times*.

Lady Llewella sat by the window with a gin and tonic and view of the racecourse. She watched her husband as he opened and examined a drawer, for the third time, and she forgot, just a little bit more, how dashing he looked on their wedding day.

"And what if he doesn't win?"

Markham favoured her a knowing smile and something just short of a wink. "He *will* win. It's a claim race, you see, and Mister Yardpole is claiming the full allowance — Spoons will be running without handicap weight."

"Yes, that's all very well and good, Markham, but it's some distance from a guarantee, isn't it." Lady Llewella plucked an edge of lime from her drink and bit it in half. "And Spoons has been very off his form lately."

"Has he?" Markham looked out the window as though hoping to catch a glimpse of the horse in question. "Do you think I ought to play him my violin?"

"I doubt it would help," said Llewella with cool, well-aimed euphemism. "What would help is if you were to withdraw Spoons from the race."

"Oh, I mustn't do that, my dear." Markham searched the drawer for a fourth time. "You see, Bitterbrook knows all about the Irish reels, somehow."

"You probably told him yourself."

"I most certainly didn't tell him myself." His Lordship gaped awed lolly eyes at his wife. "He says that it's widely known, but using his influence he's been able to contain it."

"Well, for goodness sake, Markham, how does Bitterbrook knowing about the Irish reels influence whether or not Spoons should be entered in a claim race?"

"He explains it far better than I do," confessed Markham, "but he says if Spoons does well in his first race, he'll be better able to convince the stewards that there's no cheating going on at Middleditch stables..." his eyes widened further and his voice dropped to a conspiratorial hush, "...even though there is."

"Is that what he means, Markham? Or is he simply blackmailing you into running Spoons in a claim race?"

"Blackmail?" Markham pleated his pate in thought. "No. No, I don't think he mentioned anything about blackmail. Should I ask him again, do you think?"

"Why you let him bully you so, I'll never understand." Lady Llew finished her gin and tonic with meaning.

"Oh, by the way, Teddy has asked you and Lady Olivia for nightcap cocktails," recalled Markham. "At ten o'clock, in the games room."

"With Olivia?" panicked Llewella. "It's nearly nine, now, and I have nothing to wear."

Lord Markham regarded his wife who, to his eye, appeared fully dressed.

"Oh, why don't you just go and... look for your glasses in the library," instructed Lady Llewella, and Lord Markham, judging it a sound idea, pottered off to do just that. Moments later, Lady Llewella, conspicuously wearing the very frock she'd worn at dinner and her riding boots, stole out after him, down the stairs, and out the front door.

Not twenty minutes later she encountered Stilts on the paddock.

"What ho, Lady L."

"Oh, ah, ha ha ha ha," replied Lady Llewella.

"Right oh," agreed Stilts.

"I've just been checking on the horses," claimed Lady Llewella, having regained control of herself.

"Just on my way to do the same. I'll be heading back to London, soon, where the automobile is king and any member of the noble breed of steed are almost all cart horses, and they're very rarely very matey."

"Ah ha ha ha," sympathised Llewella.

Stilts, so far as he was concerned, had spoken only the simple truth and nothing tremendously amusing, but he answered "Ha ha" because he was a good houseguest and had grown familiar by now to the unique cadence of conversation with his hostess. He then tipped his hat and wished her a good evening and waved her into the mist.

The fog had thickened such that the windows overlooking the stable and grounds had become yellow smears. Stilts reasoned that he and the racecourse were all but invisible, but nevertheless took the entirely pointless precaution of pulling his deerstalker low over his eyes and strutting noiselessly to the stable door.

The door wouldn't open. He gave the latch a casual pull and it slipped from his hand, as though someone were simultaneously pulling the opposite direction. This happened a second and then a third time and then Stilts employed his not-insubstantial height as a counter-lever. The door, this time, offered no resistance at all and so Stilts back-pedalled impressively and sat on the ground, from where he strained to focus on the dark figure in the doorway.

"Oh, uh, what ho."

Aunty Azalea stared as orb-eyed at Stilts as anyone else might at an axe-murderer. Then, slowly and as though gliding on air, she backed into the darkness.

"Oh, I say," said Stilts. "We've met, I think."

Stilts and Azalea had met, in fact, on three separate occasions, but in every case she'd been presenting as a pantomime horse or a rubber plant or something along those lines. Tonight she was dressed as Azalea Boisjoly in slate-grey tea gown and two cardigans and desperately wishing she'd taken the simple precaution of bringing along her fencing mask.

"No..." answered Azalea in a vaguely ethereal voice. "No, we haven't met. We're not meeting now."

To Azalea's dismay, Stilts followed her into the stable. "I thought I'd seen you today at Bromford Bridge."

"Oh, no," Azalea assured him. "That's my cousin, the temperance campaigner."

"Quite sure? You rather do look like her."

"We're twins."

"Oh, right." Stilts nodded simple acceptance of this, but then, knowing not what pain he wrought, said, "I thought you were cousins."

"We're twin cousins," grappled Azalea. "My mother and her mother are sisters, and our fathers are brothers."

"Oh, yes?"

"And we were born on the same day."

"Blimey."

"And we have the same name."

"Oh, I say, that's just like Trifles Tinsdale, member of my club."

"Yes," agreed Azalea. "Just like him."

"Them," corrected Stilts. "Trifles Tinsdale is actually two chaps — Bart Tinsdale and his cousin Art. Just like you and your cousin Azalea, Azalea, their mothers and aunts are sisters, and their fathers and uncles are brothers, and they look so much alike that they're able to convincingly use the same membership at the Juniper, saving a fortune in fees."

Azalea issued a sort of "Mmmp" sound that she hoped would be received as valedictorial. It wasn't.

"You're quite right," acknowledged Stilts, "but so long as they don't use the dining facilities or the bar at the same time, the club steward just assumes that Trifles is restless."

"Ah. Well. Cor. Lumme. Fancy that."

"Picked up on that, did you? Yes, you see, when I say nobody knows that Trifles is two chaps, I mean to say nobody but me," Stilts confided in this near stranger that he felt, somehow, he could trust with the secret of Trifles Tinsdale. "Bart and Art Tinsdale are practically indistinguishable — they even have a mole on their left cheeks and the precise same reaction to boiled red cabbage — but they have very different balding patterns. Bart's is perfectly circular, like a monk's tonsure, while Art's is actually two islands of bald, like Guernsey and Jersey seen from a hot air balloon. Unnoticeable at sea level, but for someone with my unique perspective — you may have noticed that I'm a bit taller than most chaps — they might as well be different colours."

As this narrative unfolded, Azalea had been inching her way imperceptibly towards the door, drawn by the cover of the evening fog which flowed through it.

"Coo…" Azalea continued drawing on a well of conversational declarations that had run dry at 'Lumme'. "…Great pip. Fiddle me that, old shoe…" This last note lingered on the air as she disappeared into the fog.

Stilts watched after her for a bit and then closed the stable door. He whistled a liberal interpretation of *Stewball* between his teeth as he wandered down the corridor to Spoons' stall.

"What ho, me ol' dipper."

Spoons regarded Stilts with pride on his forelock and a smile in his heart and a chicken on his head.

Azalea, heady with self-exaltation at the smooth diplomacy she'd employed in taking leave of Stilts, slipped with noiseless abandon through the front door of Middleditch Castle and then took casual, confident cover in the shadow of the stairs. She listened to the silence for ten brief and reassuring minutes, but the moment she put a foot on the first step she heard voices descending.

"My Schiaparelli was hung between the Doucet and the Douillet and you know that it must hang on its own in a low breeze or it loses its *vivacité*, and the sash from the Lelong diamanté designed for the opening of *The Threepenny Opera* was on the Lelong chiffon designed for closing night of *Der singende Teufel.*"

Lady Olivia Bitterbrook and her lady's maid, Alice, were locked in conversation. It's perhaps more accurate to describe them as locked in lecture as Lady Olivia reminded Alice of some of her core duties and Alice quietly meditated on the theme of pejoratives. So absorbed were they in these diversions that they passed without noticing what may have been a maid frantically polishing a newel post with a cardigan.

"Yes, madam." Alice was like Lady Olivia in that they were the exact same size of dress, shoe, glove, and hat, for purposes of expediency, should Lady Olivia need to be in two fittings at once. She was unlike Lady Olivia in every other way, and this evening wore a white-on-black pinafore dress, while Olivia was in a black-on-white pinafore-inspired dress by Jean Patou.

"I'm having drinks with Miss Quillfeather and Lady Middleditch in twenty minutes," continued Lady Olivia as they took the stairs to the ground floor, "that leaves just enough time for you to fluff the chantilly bombasts in my Jeanne Lanvin cocktail jacket."

"Yes, madam." Alice unlocked the door to Lady Olivia's ground floor wardrobe room. She turned and pulled the handle and then pulled and pulled again. "It won't open."

'It's these damp old castles..." Lady Olivia joined Alice in pulling on the door. "You're going to have to air out absolutely everything when we get back to civilisation."

The two ladies put their backs into it and the door ceded and retreated elastically, as though offering playful resistance. This gave the ladies strength of will and reckoning, and together they eased the door open in a single slow, heavy arc until it suddenly gave way entirely. Lady Olivia entered and turned on the light, revealing a rope tied to the door and running through a complex block and tackle mechanism on the window sill. This fell away almost instantly as the rope outside slackened and a moment later a wheelbarrow slid through the window and dropped onto the floor.

The wheelbarrow was followed, with immeasurably increasing speed, by a deluge of mud. It was all Olivia and Alice could do to push the door shut behind them and make their escape as the entire east garden flooded into the wardrobe room from floor to ceiling.

CHAPTER SIXTEEN

In which Spoons returns to form, Lord Markham confesses, and Teddy offers practical advice to the amateur perjurer.

THE RIBBON DROPPED and Spoons let out the clutch and dug chunks out of the racecourse, putting it behind him in a blur. The clean cold morning wind was in his face and blowing back his donkey ears as he led his herd of one, formed of his best friend in the whole world, after Chicken. Chicken didn't run, though. Chicken, Spoons felt quite sure, was too spiritual for the feral havoc and roar of the charge, and she rose above all that to a position of personal touchstone and tether, a role she currently performed with cool aplomb beneath the arm of Woolly Man.

Spoons panned the plains ahead and then glided diagonally across to the inside rail, puffing an authoritative 'this way' to that other horse — the shimmery one. The veld ahead curved out of sight but Spoons knew this length of prairieland, and with a snort he loosed himself into the straight and pistoned the field into the fleeting past.

Spoons cocked an ear for Shimmery Horse, judged the herd safe and near, and bolted over the finish line.

"It's Spoons by two leggy lengths," measured Stilts as Chockit Rockit rumbled roundly into second place in a two-horse race.

It was a cold, clear, early Midlands morning, ideal for light training and a return to form for Spoons. Teddy and Stilts watched from the paddock side of the finish line of Middleditch Racecourse while Mister Yardpole and Chicken observed from the inner circle.

"Spoons is back on his game, then." Teddy hugged a mug of black coffee and luxuriated in the brume and perfume. "What do you suppose it was put him off last week?"

"Not the chicken," said Stilts with a distracted, dimwitted air, before rethinking it and saying, "Or, to put it another way, perhaps it was the chicken."

Teddy side-eyed Stilts. "Why not the chicken, Stilts?"

"I mean to say, you said that Spoons and his chicken weren't getting on."

"Yes. Mister Yardpole and I observed a certain coolness between them during the Middleditch races when Spoons came in last."

"Well, there you go then."

"Stilts, do you recall last Christmas, when we tried to Brooklyn Bridge our way backstage at the Richmond production of *The Magic Flute?*"

"No."

"Yes you do. You claimed to be the composer."

"I thought it was Prokofiev."

"No you didn't, Stilts," Teddy reminded him. "You said that you were Mozart, and you repeated the claim the next day in court."

"Yes, very well, Teddy. Your point being?"

"You have no talent for practical perjury," explained Teddy. "You know something about Spoons and for some reason you don't want to tell me what it is."

"It's nothing sinister, Tedds." Stilts took up a Thermos flask and refilled their respective mugs of coffee. "Milk?"

"There is no milk."

"I could run back to the castle and get you some."

"No, thank you, Stilts." Teddy levelled a meaningful and proven squint on Stilts. "All my coffee wants is to know what you're on about with regards to that chicken."

"I'm merely observing that Spoons appears to have reconciled with his chicken, and has done since at least last night, when I went to check on him."

"Go on."

"Ehm, think I'm done, Tedds."

Teddy raised the intensity of her squint to a level that would be dangerous in the hands of an amateur. "Then it stands to reason that he'd be performing well now, if it was a breakdown in poultry-equine diplomatic relations that caused the initial loss of speed and focus."

"Oh, I say, that's true." Stilts nodded absently and focused hard on the next county but nevertheless felt the squint burning his cheek.

"You took Spoons for a run last night," guessed, correctly, Teddy.

"Well, dash it, Teddy, I'm every bit the horseman those chaps are." Stilts tipped an envious chin towards Flat Milliken and Pudge Hillock who, still on their respective mounts, were smiling and congratulating one another and being smugly underweight. "So something other than the stricken chicken was wrong with Spoons, because they were happy as an old married couple last night and I got nothing like the time out of him that he just now did for Pudge."

"You don't suppose it's because you're twice as heavy and three times taller?" wondered Teddy. "It would have been like running into a headwind with a ruddy great sail on his back."

"I feel I compensate for these perceived shortcomings with skill and passion," said Stilts with cool dignity.

"What if you'd broken him? Can you imagine what Lord Markham would say if you'd strained a fetlock or some such thing?"

"I didn't break him, did I, Teddy?" pointed out Stilts. "It was just a victimless bit of fun wasn't it? Not as though, as a random counter-example, I introduced a landslide into the ground floor of the north east tower."

"You did, actually." Teddy sipped her coffee and watched Spoons dressage back to the paddock with Chicken on his head. "And it was fine work, too."

"We only bogged all Lady Olivia's travel togs, is all."

"That was a happy side effect. Marshpool's letters to the parlour maid were in the wardrobe room."

"Oh, right." Stilts considered this highly mitigating feature of the crime. "Are you sure?"

"Couldn't be more sure if I'd put them there myself." Teddy toasted the vagaries of fate with the remains of her coffee and held out her cup for more. "Marshpool has already been informed that he's free to ignore the wishes of Lord Bitterbrook, breathe the blossomed air of liberty, and write exploratory propositions to the downstairs maid."

Stilts looked into the Thermos flask. "All gone."

"Then it's time for breakfast," deduced Teddy. "You coming?"

"I've had mine — talking of which, Tedds, strangest thing — I went down for breakfast with the birds this morning and yet someone was already there."

"I've heard stranger things," revealed Teddy. "I once went down for breakfast at Chipping Chase and there were two vicars thumb wrestling for the last kipper."

"No, I mean to say, there was a woman in the breakfast room whom I'd seen last night in the stables," clarified Stilts. "But then, when I issued the jovial morning 'what ho', she just turned and polished the window with her napkin."

"That's my Aunty Azalea."

"*That's* your Aunty Azalea."

"Yes, Stilts, you've met her. Several times," said Teddy. "She does have something of an acquired reflex for defensive colouration, though. I once saw her spend an entire teatime with a lampshade on her head, disguised as a floor lamp. It wasn't convincing at all — we were on a train — but everyone was very impressed by her perseverance. When you saw her in the breakfast room she was doubtless hoping to pass as the scullery."

"Does that mean you have two Aunty Azaleas?" puzzled Stilts.

"Not that I know of. I have three Uncle Georges, but who doesn't these days? Why do you ask?"

"Doesn't your Aunty Azalea have an identical cousin, also named Azalea?"

"Did she tell you that?"

"She did," confirmed Stilts. "When I told her that I thought I'd seen her at Bromford Bridge."

"That was her. She just didn't want to make conversation. What was she doing in the stables?"

"No idea, now I think of it." Stilts thought of it and then, as is so often the case, this led to him thinking more of it. "I say, you know who else was in the stables last night? Lady Llewella."

Lady Llewella sat at the tower window of the salon that joined her and Markham's bedrooms, watching Teddy and Stilts through a pair of opera glasses. She lowered the binoculars and regarded

Lord Markham, who had balanced his edition of *Track and Turf* on the chimneypiece, such that he could read it from five feet away without his pince-nez.

"Spoons is back on form, I'm pleased to say. He beat Chockit Rockit by fully two lengths."

"There you go, Lulula." Markham stepped to the mantle, turned a page of *Track and Turf,* and stepped back. "He'll win easily. Nothing to worry about."

"Well, good then, that'll only leave me not knowing what to do with all that rat poison I was going to put in your tea if you lost my horse."

A knock at the door deprived Lady Llewella of what was certainly going to be a vexingly literal reply. Lord Markham called "Come in" and Marshpool did just that.

"Good morning Your Ladyship, Your Lordship." The butler presented a silver salver. "I chanced upon your pince-nez, sir."

"Oh, I say, well done, Marshpool." Lord Markham took up the spectacles and clipped them directly on his nose. "I must get a chain for these. Where did you find them?"

"In the breakfast dining room, sir, beneath Lord Bitterbrook's napkin."

"How extraordinary. I'll be forgetting my head, next. Thank you very much, Marshpool."

"A most sincere pleasure, Your Lordship."

"Oh, I say, Marshpool." Lady Llewella's light, detached twitter disguised a ravenous curiosity. "How are the recovery operations proceeding on the ground floor?"

"Slowly, I regret to say, madam." Marshpool managed to not only keep all the regret from his voice but to in fact inflect it with a bit of playful whimsy.

"Oh, dear." Lady Llewella, despite the gravity of the tragedy, was also able to maintain a brave manner. "Poor Lady Olivia." Raised from childhood to present a noble face to adversity, Lady Lulu smiled and even giggled a little. "Can much be salvaged of her wardrobe?"

"It's perhaps a little early to say, madam." Marshpool paused to swallow hard. "When the groundsmen dredged the trench, the entire contents of two steamer trunks were caught in the tide and are now clogging the drainage culvert."

"Ha!" Lady Llewella slapped a hand over her mouth, nodded sympathetically, and said, "Ah. Oh. Oh dear."

"And..." Marshpool looked up and brushed away a tear. "And several dresses are quite infused with mud... the groundsmen stood them in the hall to dry, and now they've gone all stiff... so they.. they look like a queue of flat ladies, waiting for a bus."

Lady Llewella at this point allowed her noble resistance to misfortune completely take control in the form of a full-on belly laugh.

"You really should take a look, madam. It's a proper sight." Marshpool regained his composure and straightened his face. "And doubtless Lady Olivia would be most grateful for your concern."

"Spoons is back on form. He beat Chockit Rockit by fully two lengths."

Lady Olivia Bitterbrook reported these all-purpose tidings to Lord Stanley Bitterbrook as she returned from her bedroom, the window of which provides a view of the finish line of Middleditch Racecourse. Lord Sticky was instituting an exceptionally yet characteristically unsystematic search for Lord Markham's pince-nez.

"Well, that's certainly a relief." Sticky, struck by the potential of this development, stopped checking the inside pocket of a raincoat he hadn't been wearing. "I wonder why."

"It makes little difference," dismissed Olivia, "he's going to win regardless. Have you told Lord Markham that he mustn't make a bid at auction for Spoons?"

"No, not yet I haven't." Sticky now checked the pockets of his wife's raincoat. "Best kept to the last minute, don't you think? In case he's able to think up a way around it."

"Markham Lord Middleditch," doubted Olivia, "think up a way around something."

"No, I know, it's not terribly likely, but why take chances?"

"Because I'd prefer to not spend another minute in this swamp than absolutely necessary, that's why," explained Olivia. "My wardrobe calendar for the next two seasons is literally dead and buried. I have no idea what I'm going to do for Epsom, and after that I'll simply have to become a recluse in Paris."

"You still have all those frocks and whatnot in your room," Sticky reminded her.

Lady Olivia regarded her husband with a slow, despairing shake of the head. "I've *worn* all those. In any case, once you've told the stewards that Markham won a minor fortune on Chockit Rockit at Cheveley, I can't imagine we'll be very welcome here."

"I won't need to tell the stewards anything, though," pointed out Lord Sticky.

"But after we've won Spoons at auction, there's nothing *preventing* you from telling, either, is there?"

"No..." Sticky searched, once again, the writing desk and found, once again, Lady Brimble's damascene pince-nez. "But why would I?"

"Because then Markham will be warned off, Middleditch Stables will be ruined, and we'll have our pick of the remains for Bitterbrook Stables."

"The stewards are here, Uncle Munkle."

Teddy unleashed this announcement on an undefended library occupied by Markham Lord Middleditch and Stanley Lord Bitterbrook.

Markham remained unaffected, initially, absorbed as he was by the ceiling of the library, which was a fresco depiction of an eternal race. He'd seen the painting many times before, of course, but the painting was for him a cause of existential angst, having no start nor finish line.

Presently, the awareness that officials of the Jockey Club were without startled him into the moment. He'd been expecting this almost from the instant that Chockit Rockit had shot out of the gate at Cheveley and he realised the enormity of what he'd wrought with his violin. Nevertheless the actual eventuality, morbidly anticipated as it was, came to him as a jolt, and he spilt his tea.

"The stewards, Teddy?"

"The stewards, Uncle."

"Very well." Lord Markham rose from his club chair by the

fire, slowly but with great gravitas and resolve. "You may inform them I'll come quietly."

"I think they're happy to wait in the jockey lockey with Mister Yardpole while you sign these." Teddy raised 'these', which turned out to be a thick sheath of papers.

"What have you got there?" asked Lord Markham. "Is it a confession?"

"It's the registrations and claims for Monday's card at Bromford Bridge."

"Doesn't Mister Yardpole normally do that?" Much relieved and anxious to return to his state of sedate study of the infinite, Lord Markham poured himself a fresh cup of tea in a clean cup.

"He did do, but I took them away from him," said Teddy. "You don't think you want to have a last second thought with regards to entering Spoons in a claim race? He's been a bit off his stroke, of late."

"Yes, I see what you mean." Lord Markham, easily influenced, nodded in complete agreement.

"Also, Aunty Lulu was asking me about cyanide," added Teddy, "and I really can't spare any at the moment, what with the London mating season kicking off soon."

Lord Bitterbrook, listening to this exchange, mused on the tender ambitions of his own sweet wife, and saw them at odds with what appeared to be playing out.

"Not thinking of changing your mind, are you Markham?" asked Lord Bitterbrook with what he thought was casual disinterest but in fact sounded more like a warning of an oncoming train.

"Oh, right. No. No, not thinking of changing my mind," piffled Lord Markham. "Best hand it over, Teddy."

"Right oh," conceded Teddy, and set out the pages on the reading table.

"In that instance, you can sign all these and all." Teddy held up the rest of the papers.

"What's all that?"

"Plan B, in case Spoons doesn't win — you stake as many claims as you're allowed and you're still likely able to buy him for the claim price."

"Can't have that, Markham," emergency braked Bitterbrook.

"Not so soon after Cheveley. Give them here, Teddy — I'll stake the claims, and if for some reason Spoons doesn't win on Monday, well, I'll just sell him back to you for the asking price."

Teddy reluctantly handed over the remaining pages to Lord Bitterbrook. Lord Markham fitted his pince-nez and committed Spoons to his first claim race, but regarded his fellow peer with what was for him a rare and unwelcome sensation — growing suspicion.

Silence reigned until the autographs were complete, and then Stanley Lord Bitterbrook handed over his stack to Teddy and said, "There, now, nothing can possibly go wrong."

❦

"Something could well go wrong."

Teddy and Mister Yardpole were in the stables when she shared an apparently minor concern but was, it can be revealed, a concrete certainty — something was going to go wrong. Teddy, distracted as she was by the elaborate fresco on the ceiling of the stable, spoke in vague terms.

"Tell me again how this claiming handicap business operates?"

"Every horse except the winner is sold at the end of the race for a fixed price," explained Mister Yardpole. "The buyers are drawn from a list of those who've registered a claim, and they can decide whether or not they want the horse at the asking price."

"So I can claim a claim on a claim in a claim race," paraphrased Teddy. "Right oh."

"And every horse entered in a claim race carries the same handicapping weight. I can claim a reduction, but then the price of the horse goes down, in this case, two hundred pounds for every pound I claim."

"So, to reduce the claims on the claim horse in the claim race, we want to claim the highest handicap."

"Exactly."

"Would he win anyway?"

"Spoons is very much back on top form," judged Mister Yardpole.

"So, if we were to let him carry the full ten pounds, he'd still win, but if he didn't his claim price would go up by two thousand pounds."

"Ehm..." Mister Yardpole glanced discreetly down at his fingers.

"It's two thousand pounds," Teddy assured him. "So, just in case, let's not claim anything — Spoons can carry the full ten pounds."

"Just what I was thinking," agreed Mister Yardpole. "What you might call an *acksy-own derry-air.*"

"My thoughts precisely, Mister Yardpole — now absolutely nothing can go wrong."

CHAPTER SEVENTEEN

In which the tick-tacks scope the Silver Ring, Oy Roy charvers himself but proper and can't believe his own baby's, and Teddy pitches right porkies.

BROMFORD BRIDGE, like most racecourses, divides its enclosures by class, a policy enforced by a combination of ticket price, dress code, and eyebrows raised progressively higher in accordance with the suppliant's acquaintance with — or blood ties to — owners, nobility, or royalty.

The people's enclosure is the Silver Ring where, if a chap is wearing both shirt and trousers, he's all right. After that is the Members Enclosure, for officials, paying members and their families, and anyone clever enough to wear a top hat and tails in the Silver Ring. Then there is the Tattersalls Enclosure, named for the bloodstock auctioneer Richard Tattersall and open to owners, buyers, bidders, trainers, and the rare sportsman who found, on waking that morning, that he had too much money. There is no Royal Enclosure at Bromford Bridge, so next is the Winners Circle, the qualifications for entry of which are evident, and the Parade Circle, largely limited to horses, riders, and grown men called stable lads.

Finally and intermittently, occupying a prime corner between Tattersalls and the Winners Circle, was the Jimmy Fairly Champagne Circle. Entry was largely arbitrary and enforced by a velvet rope and stanchion barrier, like those employed in museums and galleries, operated by Somersby, who on this superb and sunny Easter Monday raised the rope for Teddy.

"What ho, Jimmy."

"Ah, Teddy." Jimmy Fairly, installed at a bistro table beneath a parasol, was dressed for a day at the races in charcoal swallowtails with matching ascot, spats, placemats, and above-mentioned parasol. "Come and have a north shore Mersea oyster. Do you prefer Sicilian lemon or Corsican?"

"Just as it comes from the tin, thanks, Jimmy." Teddy, outfitted in a pleated drop waist in British racing green, like a Ley and 6.9 litre Straight-8, but in chiffon, breezed onto the chair next to Jimmy, overlooking Tattersalls and the finish line.

Jimmy appraised her over an oyster shell. "You look like a girl with a secret."

"Well, that's just spooky, Jimmy," Teddy called it. "You're right, I am. Somersby and I are engaged, but we must keep it quiet until I can raise enough for the dowry."

"Have you worked out who the short man in the false beard is and how he's picking horses?"

' Oh, that." Teddy took up her champagne glass so that she might wave it dismissively. "Ages ago, yes. I've been occupied with other things, though, chiefly keeping a beloved horse from being lost to a claim race."

"Spoons."

"Thank you, Somersby." Teddy held out her glass for a first fill. "What are you offering on him?"

"One hundred-to-8, and lengthening as we speak."

"Blimey," calculated Teddy. "I take it Stilts told you that Spoon's been performing poorly of late."

"As I believe I mentioned, Teddy, knowledge is currency in my line of work."

"Say, that's right, it is, isn't it? So, what's that you owe me, now? One little old lady, I believe, of the sweet and grey haired variety."

"That is, indeed, the arrangement." Jimmy aimed a discreet squint between the rope barrier, where a small queue of earls and marquises was forming. "Best switch to the Veuve Clicquot, Somersby, and no refills unless they're betting more than a hundred pounds."

"But before you'll tell me what you know, you want me to tell you what I know," deduced Teddy. "This is a feature of this case, if I might employ that word, the significance of which has only struck me recently — the sheer number of sequential dependencies. To save my uncle being warned off, I have to work out who bet on Chockit Rockit to win Cheveley. To do that I have to discover the identity of the sweet little old lady, which you'll trade me for the secret of the short beardy bloke, which seems intractably connected to random disqualifications via, according to you and Oy Roy, a conspiracy."

"Exactly."

"Against Oy Roy. Or the entire industry. Or my uncle. Or a horse named Chockit Rockit, just because he changes colours in the sunshine."

"Or me."

"Or you," agreed Teddy. "But if you know who the sweet little old grey haired tout is, why don't you know the rest of the conspiracy?"

Jimmy smiled a knowing smile and nodded a knowing nod and said, "We'll have the pickled Peak quail's eggs and Durham mustard, now, Somersby. North sea salt, Teddy, or Mediterranean?"

"Let's put it in terms you'll best understand, Jimmy." Teddy finished her champagne. "I'll tell you what I know first, on the condition that you'll bet me a thousand pounds even money that you don't know who the little old lady is, and you were just bluffing in accordance with your stated policy of appearing as though you know something, even and especially when you don't."

"Ehm..."

"Okay, two thousand. I'll give you odds. You like odds, don't you?"

A general chatter and clatter arose from the polished oak bar, where Somersby was entertaining two dukes and a baroness with a seven level champagne fountain.

Jimmy profited from the distraction to reflect before saying, "I don't know who the little old lady is."

"I know you don't, Jimmy, but I do." Teddy checked Jimmy's pending motion with a raised hand while she paid respect to another glass of champagne. "I'm not going to tell you. That's for Oy Roy. However for a short time only but on excellent terms, I am able to offer you one short, bearded punter with precognition."

"Terms?"

"Which you must respect, even when it turns out that the answer was obvious all along."

"Is it obvious?"

' It's astonishing how many people seem to think so, after it's been explained." Teddy pushed aside an antique terracotta vase of Cornish winter wheat bread sticks, creating a clear and level playing field. "Short beardy punter is a jockey."

"He's never a jockey," scoffed Jimmy. "Jockeys never bet."

"Jockeys never bet on the horses they ride," clarified Teddy. "Short beardy punter is a jockey, but he's not always the same jockey. Oy Roy tells me that the only power in the universe that can hold back or, in close corollary, choose *not* to hold back a horse, is a jockey, and so there you go — the only people who can know the winner are the jockeys. They decide the result of the occasional race and whichever among them isn't riding glues on a beard and becomes your never-miss punter."

Jimmy considered this proposition with a frown so deep that Somersby, misinterpreting the expression, cut off an earl.

"Furthermore," furthered Teddy more, "short beardy punter was here on Friday, but our surveillance team determined that he didn't come through the front gate. That leaves only those who arrived with the horses — the owners, the trainers, and the jockeys."

"If the jockeys are fixing some races..." wondered Jimmy, for he was not a man who readily understood limits, "...why don't they fix all the races?"

"What makes you think they don't? They may well be placing bets through other means and with other bookies. It was certainly Flat Milliken and Pudge Hillock who arranged for Chockit Rockit to have such long odds going into Cheveley."

"You think so?"

"Once again — no one else could have done it, and I know that Uncle Markham didn't ask them to."

"So, the jockeys are operating a complex, cross-track conspiracy in complete secrecy, with no one twigging."

"No, they're operating a complex, cross-track conspiracy with no one twigging but me. Still, very clever and very discreet." Teddy toasted the restraint and quiet living for which jockeys are famous with the last of her champagne. "Don't forget the terms — you cannot act on this information. Just keep taking short beardy man's bets, if he makes any, and leave the rest to me — I have a plan."

The Silver Ring is the natural habitat of the blue-breasted British bookie. They perch on milking stools or upturned buckets, crowing their call of best odds, prompt payment, and honest dealings. Their plumage, on race days, is at its brightest and most alluring, and has evolved to compete for the attention of the domestic racing pigeon.

The Silver Ring bookies position themselves several yards apart with a chalkboard on which they mark the ever-shifting odds of the next fixture on the card.

This is where Teddy found Oy Roy, standing on a soap box in bookie-boots for a total increase in height of just over a foot and a half. In the moment, he was watching one of his tick-tack men at the far end of the field of bookies, communicating by secret hand-signs the odds being offered by Honest John Tupping, Honest Bob Telford, and Earnest Earnest Dalderby.

"Clock me, Teddy." Oy lowered his spyglasses and shook his head in despair. "I've charvered meself well and good, I have. Can't pick me own slips without me tick-tack rucking every other bookie in the ring."

Teddy clocked Oy Roy. Even his wardrobe was a shadow of the former flamboyance, and his mauve and orange checked jacket very nearly matched his mauve and white (left leg mauve, right leg white) trousers. His yellow tie looked mainly like a yellow tie as the sunshine muted the effect of the pattern of little golden portraits of the king. His pink derby with a George flag stemming from the hat band looked like just the sort of pink derby that would be worn to the races by a respected judge, or the Archbishop of Canterbury.

"What'll you give me on Spoons in the sixth?" asked Teddy.

"He's got no brief, Teddy. An unknown commodity, what's never raced before, which means I'm not allowed to know that he's rumoured to have lost his bottle, and am in a position to offer you 30-to-7."

"Blimey."

"Blimey would be the dicky, Teddy, if I'd given you odds, which I didn't."

"Right oh, well, if and when you do, you can do so with your old confidence and cool." Teddy stepped closer to form a zone of shared secrets. "I know who your sweet little old track tout is, and how she's doing it."

Oy took off his apple green, lime green, tangerine, and byzantine quiltwork scarf and hung it over his tote board. He stepped down from his soap box and led Teddy to the comparative privacy of the rail.

"Who is she?"

"Oy, have you ever seen this little old lady?"

"Never set baby's on her."

"No. And has Chard ever set eyes on her?"

"He has not."

"None of us have, Oy," pointed out Teddy. "In fact, we have only the word of some decidedly naive punters that the tout is, in fact, a little old lady."

"Why would they say she was if she wasn't?" asked Oy with surprising clarity.

"I've little doubt they think she's a little old lady," said Teddy. "But any short chap in a grey wig, a church frock, and a morning-after voice is going to convince a punter who really wants to believe he's onto a good and exclusive thing."

Oy nodded like a man coming willingly to the light.

"But, why? Why not just slip them the griffin?"

"Why does anyone put on a disguise, Oy?" asked Teddy. "They don't want to be recognised. In fact, they couldn't afford to be."

"They?" Oy removed his hat and placed it over his heart. "The jockeys."

"They're fixing races and placing bets directly with Jimmy Fairly's leg men," said Teddy. "And muddying the waters by giving winning tips to random punters."

"Diabolical..." Oy's words were marked with the stark dark heart of betrayal, with just a soupçon of admiration, "and dead clever. You think they did for Chockit Rockit?"

"Of course," confirmed Teddy. "And they're behind the seemingly random disqualifications, too. Probably got weights in their pockets or some such thing during weighing out and they pitch them onto the track during the race."

"That's bold as stewed stewards, that is."

"Talking of stewards, Oy," Teddy lowered her voice to a frequency known to be inaudible to stewards, "I think we can agree that it would be scandalous were this situation to be placed in the hands of the secular arm."

"Oh, right — it would be napoo for the lot of us." Oy put on his hat so that he might once again remove it and place it over his heart. "But what's to be done?"

"Nothing, Oy. You just carry on maintaining a low profile, and making book and taking bets, even and especially from anyone claiming to be guided by a sweet little old grey haired lady," advised Teddy. "Just leave everything in the hands of Quillfeather and Associates — we have a plan."

"Did you tell them that short beardy chap and sweet little old lady are jockeys in disguise?"

Stilts put this debrief to Teddy from his side of a barrel table and a pint of bitter in the beer garden, from where he had been watching Aunty Azalea deflect attention, this time disguised as a charity worker, soliciting donations.

"I did," Teddy assured him.

"And they believed it."

"They did, yes."

"Even though it's twaddle."

"What other explanation is there?" posited Teddy. "No suspects were seen entering the racecourse, no one else could have known the winners to specific races — who could it be but the jockeys?"

"And you told them that you had a plan, and they agreed to carry on as usual," marvelled Stilts.

"Of course they did, Stilts." Teddy finished her pint. "Now, let's expose the real short beardy punter and sweet little old grey haired tout."

CHAPTER EIGHTEEN

Which celebrates the unifying powers of on-course gambling, and gin.

"I NEVER SAID that I *wasn't* a track tout, dear."

Aunty Azalea mounted this indomitable defence from behind her deterrent to social interaction — a sandwich board. This particular sandwich board was ingeniously contrived to repel all interest inviting, as it did, the public to contribute to a charitable fund. As a further measure, the aim of the fund was to assist members of the House of Lords in offsetting the cost of accommodation while in London. Azalea also wore a kerchief that made her look like a potato vendor, and smoked glasses that made her look like a potato vendor who cheats at cards.

"Your Aunty Azalea is the sweet little grey haired old lady?" Stilts removed his hat and gazed upon this prodigy with awe. "Ask her who she likes in the second race."

"And I didn't say you were a track tout, Aunty", corrected Teddy. "You're merely the brains of the operation. Shall we discuss this in your lair?"

Azalea ducked out from beneath her sandwich board and, leaving a copper cauldron to collect any absentee donations, she accompanied Teddy and Stilts into the tea tent.

"I should have worked it out during the Middleditch fête, when you were sharing a pantomime horse costume and there were five tea ladies, and then when you were just half a horse and there were six." Teddy laid out the preliminaries while Stilts collected a tea tray, having gained Teddy's sworn oath to reveal nothing of material value until he returned.

Presently, he did just that, with a pot of cold water, crumbled scones, and almost completely clear clotted cream.

"Sorry that took so long — the water nearly boiled, so they had to let it cool before making the tea." Stilts distributed the cups. "Skipping the preliminaries, Azalea — may I call you Azalea? Have you a title you prefer, such as maestro or professor? Just tell me how you do it, and how I can, too."

"She doesn't do it, Stilts," replied Teddy on behalf of her aunt who, in any case, was affecting to appear distracted by reassembling a scone.

"She does, though," argued Stilts. "How else do you explain all those chaps picking winners out of long shots?"

"Do you recognise my Aunty Azalea, Stilts?"

"Of course I do. We met Saturday night, in the stables."

"But you saw her before that, here at Bromford Bridge, didn't you?" steered Teddy. "In fact you saw her right here in the tea tent."

"I say, that's right, I did," recalled Stilts. "When I was with that Collin chap — he didn't recognise her, though."

"That was the point, wasn't it Aunty A? Stilts saw you when he came in here with Collin because you were filling in for the sweet little old grey haired tea lady track tout who told him to bet on Shropshire Lass in the first."

Wide-eyed, Stilts scanned the smiling, apple-cheeked faces of the tea ladies.

"One of the tea ladies is the tout?" He returned his attention to the table and spoke in hushed tones. "Is it Dora? There's a certain cagey cynicism about the way she handles that piping bag, don't you think?"

"It's not one of the tea ladies, Stilts. It's all of them."

Stilts paused his cup near the end of its long journey from the saucer, and then slowly turned, cup and all, to appraise once again the gallery of sweet little old grey haired tea ladies. When he returned, he returned a wiser man.

"Ah."

"Yes," confirmed Teddy. "Oldest trick in racing, right after being Irish. One by one, each tea lady takes a break, finds a novitiate, doubtless clutching his little stake in both hands, and gives him a different tip for the next race. Of six tips, one is likely to pay out, and when it does — and only when it does — the punter puffs about it to anyone who'll listen, creating the impression that one tea lady picks a winner every time."

"Then the applicable tea lady finds the punter and, with this deal-baited, steel-plated credibility, she sells him another tip for a share of his winnings," concluded Stilts.

"Exactly."

Stilts stared hard thoughts into his cup of disappointment.

' Do we have to drink this? I could nip over to the beer garden, or nick a horse bucket. Either would be a marked and memorable improvement."

"The bad tea is intentional, I think." Teddy surveyed the terrain of the tray which, in addition to everything else, lacked spoons. "When they're working the track they can't afford to have a lot of punters coming into the tea tent looking for tea, can they? So it's deliberately awful."

"That would certainly explain it," agreed Stilts. "So, they can't predict winners."

"They cannot."

"How did you work it out, Tedds?"

"Once I realised that it was a fraud, it became obvious," explained Teddy. "And it was clearly a fraud — if the sweet little old grey haired lady could really pick winners, she'd bet them herself."

"I wouldn't," pointed out Azalea.

"No, well, you've always been a wildcard, Aunty, but the point stands — the multiple tip scam works best with multiple tippers pointing, once again, to the tea ladies."

"Why not some other sweet grey haired old lady?" Stilts wanted to know.

"We're at the track, Stilts, the only little old ladies are literally the tea ladies, narrowing down the suspects considerably," said Teddy. 'And yet, Collin didn't recognise any of them. You did, though, and at a moment when Aunty Azalea had abandoned her post as temperance campaigner. Why would they need to resort to the extreme measure of putting Aunty Azalea on the front line like that, except to prevent Collin from recognising his tout?"

Stilts brooded on this conclusive summation. "Well, I won't say I'm not disappointed."

"I'm not," said Teddy. "On the contrary, I'm delighted. I didn't know you had it in you, Aunts."

"I do like a flutter," admitted Azalea in a wary whisper. "It's the people I can't stick. Betting seems to make people so loud and... oh..."

"Sociable?" suggested Teddy.

"Sociable." Azalea repeated the indictment for the benefit of an invisible jury. "So I contrived a way of gambling without having to talk to bookmakers or anyone at all, really."

"Is it gambling, though, Aunty? You're not risking any money and you can never lose."

"I find that winning money is really the only bit of gambling that I enjoy."

"There's the risk of getting caught, I suppose," suggested Stilts.

"Doing what?" asked Teddy. "Touting isn't illegal, especially not the way the tea ladies do it. The perfect crime is no crime at all."

"So, we don't need to stop," concluded Azalea.

"On the contrary, Aunty Slanty — you need to step up operations," said Teddy, "and tell all your customers to put their shirts on Spoons in the fourth."

❦

As a conductor of boys choirs, Vicar Bittles was of the capacious, energetic, fully-engaged school. He liked and, more importantly, felt it aided in the development of his charges, to immerse himself in the spirit and circumstance, and not draw the line short of acrobatics, if the piece called for it.

In the moment, inspiring the boys to the best that can be got from *Quem pastores laudavere,* he appeared to be performing a particularly demanding course of military calisthenics, especially designed to improve upper body strength. In aid of that he had removed his herringbone coat and was conducting in his shirtsleeves and a sleeveless jumper, one of several made for him by the Saint Paul's and All Angels whist and knitting club.

"What ho, Vic." Teddy, appearing suddenly at Vicar Bittles' side, deftly dodged a timely instruction to the baritone section.

"Good afternoon, Miss Quillfeather. What a delight to see you here."

"You too," returned Teddy. "It's not a little blasphemous, though, ministering at the Easter Monday races?"

"There are more sincere prayers said here and now than in most churches at Christmas, Miss Quillfeather." The vicar wound down *Quem pastores laudavere* with a vigorous flutter, like a good man trying to get something sticky off his hands. "And it's an excellent location for the collection plate — anyone who doesn't make a donation on the way in is sure to make one on the way out, whether he's had a good day at the races or, even moreso, if he hasn't."

"I'll just bet they are." Teddy surveyed the choir, all dressed in silk cassocks as white as a cloud and as maintained as a parachute. "I suppose that explains the improvements to the church."

"People have been most generous." Vicar Bittles, shifting up a gear, launched the boys into *Let the Bright Seraphim* with a vigorous two-handed orchestration that looked like an Italian man complaining about soup.

"And the reflecting pool, the floral sundial..."

"The good Lord has inspired charity in many hearts."

"The Reubens..."

"Many, many hearts."

"It's nothing to do with collecting casual racing tips from Lady Fitterbrook and Lady Middleditch, then, and getting choir boys to back them in false whiskers?"

"Oh, ehm..." At this point a soprano solo was called for, and so Vicar Bittles raised his hands above his head and stood on his toes and made an 'ooooooo' face, affording him a moment to consider his answer, which of course could only be, "Yes, it's also a bit of that."

Vicar Bittles left Teddy for a moment to conduct the boys in an ambitious finale to *Let the Bright Seraphim*, sung as a three part round and requiring the vicar to function, in effect, as three different conductors sharply disagreeing on tempo.

"The stewards don't know about it, do they?" Bittles asked upon catching his breath. "It's just I've got this rather spiffing tip on the fourth race."

"Not yet, they don't. For the moment, it's between you and me — I've had a tip of my own."

"Oh?" Vicar Bittles, in a sharp shift in the programme, started the lads off on the comparatively undemanding *For All the Saints Who from Their Labours Rest*, allowing him to conduct with one hand and the 'invisible chalkboard' mime, standby of all choir masters with something on their minds. "What tip would that be?"

"Initially, it was the sacking of Chard the not-a-leg-man from the choir, for outgrowing his cassock," recalled Teddy. "But I suspect you knew that he would be an unreliable dupe in your new gambling syndicate."

"A most precocious lad."

"And then there was the big bet on Chockit Rockit," Teddy continued reading evidence into the record. "The short beardy punter was confident enough that he was going to win Cheveley to put fifty quid on it. You got that tip from Lady Llewella, who got it from Lord Markham."

"She all but forced it on me."

"But the tell was the disguise," continued Teddy. "The purpose of the beards, obviously, is to conceal the involvement of Saint Paul's and All Angels in sports betting and in particular your use of the inside information with which Lady Olivia and Lady Lulu try to buy your attention, but the result was to throw suspicion on the only other short people who could possibly need a disguise — the jockeys."

"Oh dear." Distracted, the vicar was really just twirling a finger in the air, and the altos had begun teasing the sopranos, as they will. "That was wholly unintentional, I assure you."

"And no harm was done, Vicar. Firstly, I knew that there was no way that the jockeys would risk the only livelihoods for which they're qualified, so it must have been some other short chap who needed a disguise, and that, according to our surveillance on Friday, left only the choir boys. Secondly, though, you only ever bet on horses belonging to Lord Middleditch or Lord Bitterbrook."

"Their Ladyships would continuously reveal stable secrets," acknowledged the vicar. "I could only interpret it as a sign from God."

"It's not a tiny bit forbidden in the big book of rules, Vic? Involving children in track-side wagering?"

"Not specifically — I've checked." Conducting had diminished to the point that the vicar was essentially waving at the boys, and the sopranos had taken to singing their own lyrics to the refrain, directed at the altos; 'Hallelujah, ya baboon ya, how I wish I never knew ya'. "And it's all in such a good cause — I don't know if you knew Saint Paul's and All Angels prior to my arrival, but it was pos_tively provincial. No heating, no third octave on the organ, no roof budget…"

"No Dutch masters in the nave."

'Not even one."

"And you couldn't stop Lady Olivia and Lady Llewella from vying for your attention, so you decided instead to direct their energies to good works."

'Extremely well put, Miss Quillfeather." In acknowledgement of what Vicar Bittles felt was a perfect meeting of minds, he called upon the choir to return their absolute best *Be Not Afraid*, which they only managed to do with the aid of his vivid impersonation of a man treading deep and dangerous waters.

"One thing, Vicar — that spiffing tip, was it Spoons to win in the fourth?"

"Paying as much as 18-to-1," confirmed Vicar Bittles, now exercising his elbows like an early effort at flight. "You're not going to tell me it's wrong, are you? I got it from both Lady Olivia *and* Lady Llewella."

"No, it's a good tip, Vic, and what's more I want you to back it, with everything you've got in the fund."

Spoons, so far as he could recall, had never been anxious. In point of fact, he'd been anxious on countless occasions but he was gifted with exceptionally selective memory and instantly forgot all but the most agreeable moments, so the nervous warble rising from that bit that usually tells him when he's hungry was, in the moment, new and novel and wholly unwelcome.

Much of what was going on was familiar — there was a chap on his back and a herd quorum of, he guessed, somewhere between six and six hundred cracking mates on either side, there were throngs of shouty people, a plumb and level flatland stretching out before them, and a sunny day for whatever it was he was once again about to do. The chap on his back, however, wasn't Sing-Songy Man. Instead of a ribbon he was in a stall and behind a gate. The herd struck him as a bit standoffish and nervy and, in one case, a little spitty. The shouty people were louder and more numerous than he knew that shouty people could be, and he'd never seen this track before. This was the most worrying aspect of it all, because Chicken, he knew, was watching, and this meant, to his uncomplicated reasoning, that he must assume a leadership role.

Then the gate clacked out of existence and Spoons was tread and stride aside the herd as though they'd all snapped into existence at full speed. They clomped great clumps out of the course and they thumped and thudded and thundered in a single mass of unbound horsepower into the infinite wend.

Spoons was, as Spoons always was, in the moment. Something eluded him, though. Something on his visceral to-do list, manifested as a sort of brain tickle. It felt as though he was meant to be doing something in addition to the only thing that mattered... something quite important... leading! He was meant to be leading the herd. What must the others be thinking, he would have thought, had he facility and utility for thought.

Beyond the herd the field wound out of sight and so, in accordance with Spoons' rudimentary understanding of physics, he was on the wrong side of an estimated two thousand horses. He was bounding along near the outside rail, and the shouty people blurred past as though on wheels. Where was Chicken? Chicken was typically among but apart from the shouty people, with Woolly Man. Where was Woolly Man? What was this tickle in his brain trying to tell him? It was urgent... pressing... leading! He was meant to be leading the herd and to do that he needed to angle for the inside rail.

The cannonade burst out of the curve and onto the straight and galloped abreast like a rolling storm. Spoons knew without knowing that there was little time left to assume the lead before this glorious stampede would stop. He squinted and pressed and found his path and went into the final curve near the inside rail. Still something held him back like a damp burden and he entered the final straight some five horses from his natural position as guide through these unknown lands. The herd, some ten thousand strong, would surely be lost.

An electric urgency coursed through his legs as the grazing range approached but still he was behind, now four horses, now three... where was Chicken? There! There was chicken... Two horses...

CHAPTER NINETEEN

Wherein is recounted the parable of the Nobleman and the French Customs Inspector.

THE ATMOSPHERE in the Tattersalls Enclosure was a dignified reserve. Lady Olivia and Lord Sticky shared a knowing, confident sidebrow flutter. Lady Llewella focussed a scalding squint at Lord Markham to which he remained smilingly indifferent. Teddy was filling what turned out to be a considerable lull in business at the bar to compare the effervescence, bouquet, and elusive element of tizzy-wizziness of Bollingers, Taittinger, and Moet & Chandon.

This island of isolated calm contrasted considerably with the blare and ballyhoo from the grandstand crowd who, profiting from the advantage of an unrestricted view, cheered the field on to what sounded a tight finish.

Lady Olivia and Lord Bitterbrook, Lady Llewella and Lord Markham, and Teddy, unable to actually see the finishing post, listened to what had suddenly become a sweeping silence. A rushed hush like this always meant a blanket finish — so close they could throw a blanket over win, place, and show.

A crackle, a buzz, and the tin toned tannoy announced, "And it's Spoons by a short head, followed by Hair Loom and Elmer's Bequest."

A wave of winning wagers whelmed over Tattersalls in a roar.

❦

"There, you see, my darling?" Lord Markham drew his wife's attention, in case she'd missed it, to the happy result. "Spoons has won."

"It's very lucky for you he did, Markham." This was most decidedly true. "I'm not sure what I should have done if he hadn't." This, however, was most decidedly not true.

"I'll just go and have a word with the Tattersalls man, and let him know that I'll match plus a pound the next highest bid."

"There, you see? Spoons has won."

This time it was Lady Olivia reporting common knowledge to Lord Bitterbrook, who nevertheless enjoyed hearing it.

"I'll just pop over and let the Tattersalls man know that I'll beat any bid."

"Do that," agreed Lady Olivia, "but first let Markham know that if he bids you'll tell the stewards about his bet on Cheveley and have him warned off for life."

"Oh, right, yes, I must attend to that," twigged Sticky. "Oh, I say, Markham. A word, if you please."

In the Winners Circle Pudge Hillock was sliding out of the saddle of victory and into the throng of admiration. Corks popped and bulbs flashed and there was much commotion and, above all, distraction. On the other side of the horse, the lanky stable boy unfastened the saddle and tipped it into his arms. With a deft flick of thumb and forefinger, he unhooked the pockets on either side of the saddle. He waited and then waited a moment more. He gave the saddle a discreet but vigorous shake. He waited a bit more, and then stared cow-eyed at the ground where five pounds of buckshot should have fallen and where they very noticeably did not. He shook the saddle much less discreetly. Nothing. The saddle contained no hidden weight that he could release before the weighing in, and so the winner would not be disqualified.

"It's all very simple."

Teddy made this bold claim from the presiding position of a crowded table in the tea tent, hosting a happy party of six. The tea ladies had closed for the day and the calm exclave was even calmer than usual. A light, slight rain had marked the end of the last race of the day, and had by now become a comforting, wind-rushed staccato on the canvas roof.

"I'll give you a weighty nun it isn't one bit simple," offered Oy Roy.

The seed of doubt planted, it was soon nurtured by Chard and Vicar Bittles, and possibly eventually by Stilts, but he was doing duty at the beer garden. Aunty Azalea's reaction was largely concealed by her charity worker camouflage, as she had grown accustomed to the social barriers afforded by a sandwich board, and had taken to wearing it everywhere. Oy, too, had assumed a low profile after collecting and paying out on a good day's sport, and was now wrapped in a unimposing Inverness in blue, green, yellow, and puce plaid (the tartan of clan McClown, he likes to call it), and he'd traded out his bookie boots for red Wellies that went up to his knees. Chard, mainly to obscure his age, wore low over his eyes a trilby that he'd won off a Bun Hill senior boy on the result of a hotly contested Latin quiz. Vicar Bittles was dressed as a vicar who'd been on his feet all day.

"Let's say it's no more complicated than, say, a six-horse accumulator," Teddy assured the assembly. "In fact, similar to an accumulator, the key is approaching the mysteries in the right order."

"We wasn't approaching no mysteries in any order at all, Miss," pointed out Chard.

"Well, then, follow along — to save my uncle I had to find out who nobbled Chockit Rockit and how, which meant finding out who placed the big bet on Chockit Rockit to win Cheveley, and to do that I had to sort out who might have been the sweet little old grey haired tout, and to do that I had to identify the short, beardy punter, and all that led to the mystery of the disqualified longshots."

Stilts, at this moment, returned from the bar. He was wearing inevitably undersized riding silks and holding in two hands a record-matching three pints, two whiskies, and, owing to Chard having not yet achieved the age of majority, a small brandy and soda.

"Where were we?"

"I was just about to recount the instructional parable of the Nobleman and the French Customs Inspector," claimed Teddy, "in aid of clarifying things."

"Oh, right."

"You know Bins Llannybidder, don't you, Stilts?" Teddy relieved him of her pony of whisky. "Six litre short chassis Minerva AK, until he took a wrong turn off Camden High Street into Regents Canal."

"I know Nardo Lord Llannybidder," counter-offered Stilts. "Invented what he calls higher tea — one part gin, and that's it. Serves eighty."

"That's the ·chap," confirmed Teddy. "Well, Lord Llannybidder's first-born understudy, The Honourable Bins, struck Mama as an ideal match for a girl approaching her late twenties without a worry line..."

"The Llannybidder gentlemen are of remarkably average height," piqued Stilts.

"They are," agreed Teddy. "Famous for it. They're also wealthy nobility and there's a bishop or Lord Mayor or something in the family, and so naturally Mama extorted me into joining the Llannybidder's weekend yacht trip to Le Touquet — threatened to take my motor away, again."

"Not the Invicta."

"Yes, but to be fair Mama threatens to impound Vicky once a quarter. At Christmas she promised to sell her if I appeared in the paper even one more time in the Court Proceedings section and yet we're still together, three Soho raids and one Boat Race Night later."

"Perhaps she didn't notice," suggested Stilts.

"She makes out not to, but I know for a fact that she was contacted by *The Times* for a comment after the fire brigade rescued those nuns from the roof of Harrods."

Vicar Bittles' contagious calm took the floor. "This is all most instructional, Miss Quillfeather, but does your car relate in some fashion to the sequence of mysteries at hand?"

"Allegorically, Vicar, yes, it does." Teddy steadied her pipes with a whistle of whisky. "The parable of the Nobleman and the French Customs Inspector, you see, has it that I made a gift of this concession to Mama and joined the party at Eastbourne, from whence we made our way across the channel to Le Touquet for a weekend of sailing, golfing, and The Honourable Bins hiccoughing at me."

"The cad," Stilts judged.

'That was the extent of his conversation, actually, except for a whooping soprano when all the golf balls escaped on the main deck in rough seas. Only an hour out of port and I was already glad I'd come."

"Yes, all right, that does sound quite unmissable," begrudged Stilts.

"And it only got better from there."

' Le Touquet can be quite jolly," Stilts raised his pint to French coastal villages, "even and, in my case at least, especially if one doesn't golf."

"It can be," agreed Teddy, "but we never made it to Le Touquet. Owing to a minor but meaningful mixup in the mapping department, we docked at Le Tréport, a charming little oyster bed some fifty miles to the south."

"Is that the place with a honking great casino out of which I was chucked for resting my whisky on the head of some nibs?"

"You're thinking of Monte Carlo. The nibs in question was His Serene Highness Prince Louis II of Monaco," Teddy reminded him. "But Le Tréport was not without its larks and jinks, too. For starters, Lord Nardo and The Honourable Bins didn't realise straight away that we'd pitched up at the wrong dock, and so they went on ahead to reserve a tee-off time with minimal French and poor directions. Lord Nardo was subsequently arrested for making inappropriate proposals to a net-mender, whom he'd asked where a chap could go to get some time on the fairway."

"Blimey."

"And of course, this drew the attention of the local authorities to the presence of a three-deck British-flagged schooner tied up in a tiny French fishing village, inviting interested enquiries from a French customs inspector."

"I was wondering when he was going to be introduced," said the vicar, who liked a fair distribution of roles in his parables.

"Late but pivotal," Teddy recounted. "The yacht hadn't been properly moored, it turned out, so by the time the thin blue line between France and whatever it is one could possibly want to smuggle into France from England arrived to search the boat, it had floated away."

"What became of it?" worried Vicar Bittles.

"Last seen in Belgian waters," recalled Teddy. "So they just bought a new one. First, though, Lady Llannybidder dashed off an uncharacteristically unambiguous cable to Mama, informing her that The Honourable Bins was no longer on the menu at the Quillfeather debutante ball. Turns out, she had somehow got it into her head that it was I who had released the golf balls onto the deck, altered the maritime charts to direct us to Le Tréport, urged the gentlemen to go looking for a golf club in an oyster fishery, and loosened the yacht from its moorings."

"Oh my good shepherd," ghast the vicar, scandalised on Teddy's behalf. "Why would she think such a thing?"

"To be fair, Vicar, she probably assumed," suggested Stilts. "I know I did."

"I have something of a reputation for sabotaging Mama's efforts to marry me off," admitted Teddy. "And the case for the prosecution only improved on news that I had friends in Le Tréport, who were able to give me a lift to Deauville. It looked as though I'd arranged it."

"Didn't you?" doubted Stilts.

"This brings us to the point of the parable," taught Teddy. "I didn't, but it served my purposes to allow it to be assumed that this string of unconnected mishaps was part of a well-conceived and executed anti-nuptial operation. Good for my reputation, if nothing else."

"It was all just coincidence? Even the golf balls?"

"Well, no, in point of fact, they were all separate and isolated events, but they were also all down to the fact that Nardo Lord Llannybidder, as you pointed out, puts gin in everything, including gin," explained Teddy. "Just out of port, he decided to practice his drive by knocking a few balls into the Channel, and instead upturned an entire crate of the things."

"Oh, I say," envied Stilts.

"As you should," agreed Teddy. "It was spectacular. It was like a mass release of white mice, with percussion. And of course Lord Nardo fancies himself a navigator, which he might well be if he ever tried it sober, but as it was he couldn't bring the charts sufficiently into focus to distinguish Le Touquet from Le Tréport. It was he who moored the yacht to the satisfaction of a drunken lord, and it was his idea to go off looking for a golf course."

"And your friends in town?" checked Stilts. "That was just a coincidence?"

"No, that was a judicious fabrication. I met them for the first time at a little café in port, but allowed Lord Nardo and The Honourable Bins and, by extension, Lady Llannybidder, to believe that I'd arranged to meet them there."

"But what, if I might ask, Miss Quillfeather, was the point?" Vicar Bittles, even for a choir boy Fagan, liked his parables to have a solid moral foundation.

"Of the fib, Vic, or the parable?" Teddy rendered the question rhetorical with a say-no-more hand. "The answer's the same either way — there's sometimes value in making disconnected events appear to be elements of a larger conspiracy."

"Has this brought us back to the mysteries to hand, then?" hoped Vicar Bittles.

"Once I'd worked out the case of the sweet little old grey haired track tout and, consequently, that there was no conspiracy, the rest was easy. It meant, for one thing, that short beardy punter had to be a jockey, which we knew he wasn't, or a choir boy."

"A most untrustworthy class of cove, in my experience," contributed Chard.

"And it revealed another, even more intriguing truth," Teddy paused a suspenseful glass beneath a dramatic nose. "It told me who was behind the seemingly random disqualifications." She took a cliffhanging whif of whisky. "The only person who stood to benefit." She sloshed a momentous and meaningful mouthful, swallowed a significant sip, and said, "Jimmy Fairly."

"Not at a thousand-to-1," differed Oy Roy.

"He's a bookie, Tedds," pointed out Stilts. "You'll more likely find a race-fiddling vicar. No offense intended, Vicar."

"No, fair enough." Vicar Bittles nodded in pious acquiescence, and thought of taking on a second curate to take up the slack in the parish clerk's office.

"How does Jimmy Fairly gain from everyone thinking there's a conspiracy?" Oy asked Teddy.

"Remind me what you do, Oy, when you get a concentration of longshot bets."

"I lay them off."

"You lay them off," repeated Teddy for the court. "Specifically, you place those same bets with Jimmy Fairly and he lays them off again with other bookies outside the immediate circle. That way, if the longshot wins, you collect from Jimmy, he collects on his bets, and the pain is shared, like insurance."

"Sure as."

"And what would he do with those bets, Oy, if Jimmy could know for sure that the longshot, if he won, would be disqualified?"

Oy, Stilts, and Chard, as one, stared starkly into a world they'd prefer not know.

"Never." All three said some variation of this. All three failed to convey anything like conviction.

"He never laid off the bets, Oy, because he knew he'd never have to pay out." Very much in line with the school of thought that advises the quick removal of bandages, Teddy added, "Knowledge is currency to Jimmy, and if you can't know which long shot is going to win, the second best thing to know is that it won't."

Oy, Chard, and Stilts shared pained, empty, traumatised, glassy gazes, like three kittens learning, simultaneously, that Father Christmas is known to the police.

Oy gave it voice. "What's to be done?"

"Nothing at all." Teddy took up her pony glass. "It's been done."

"What's been done, Tedds?" asked Stilts.

"The fourth race. Spoons came in at... what did he come in at, Oy?"

"A hundred-to-8."

"And did you lay it all off on Jimmy?"

"Plus five hundred nicker of me own." Oy spoke with rising surmising. "A dozen punters were putting their shirts on Spoons on account of a little old lady track tout, and because you said her tip was a sure thing."

"As it turned out to be," confirmed Teddy. "And you, Vicar?"

"Oh, uhm... I'm not sure I recall..." Vicar Bittles sought guidance from above. "Two hundred each way, with a safety hundred to show, I believe, so say a conservative 10-to-1."

"And Spoons weren't disqualified," observed Chard.

Teddy nodded. "Arrangements were made. The plan had been

to dump his weights before weighing out, but Pocket Change — registered to run as Spoons — wasn't carrying any weight."

"Who was meant to do the dumping out?" asked Stilts.

"The stable lad. Who else?" replied Teddy. "Last Friday, after Loosey Lacey was disqualified for weighing out light, there were pellets in the Winners Circle and stuck in Chockit Rockit's hoof. Someone dumped them out of the saddle after the race."

"But how do you know it was the stable lad?"

"Because it wasn't *just* the stable lads," said Teddy. "Scads of disqualifications were down to bad paperwork — wrong name, wrong owner, wrong qualifying conditions, wrong race — most of that couldn't have been the stable lads, some of the owners had to be involved, too, except the owners couldn't benefit from it. Unless, that is, they were getting payouts from a bookie, disguised as winnings. We know from the story of Sinjin Lord Ashby that owners much prefer to make their money from gambling owing to a strong, negative reaction to income tax."

"How does that reckon?" Chard wanted to know. "A punter can't bet on a horse to lose."

"No, but a bookie can," said Teddy. "In fact, that's what bookies do. My guess is that the owners who disqualified their horses were paid their share in retroactive bets placed on the eventual winner. Illegal, maybe, but entirely untraceable."

"Diabolical." Oy tried and failed to draw solace from his pint.

"It's enough to destroy a lad's faith." Chard finished his brandy in a single throw.

"A stain on the noblest of professions." Stilts made a bitter toast of bitter.

"Unthinkable," Vicar Bittles returned the toast. "Why, it would be like an insurance company accepting premiums with no intention of ever honouring a claim."

"On the other hand…" Oy idly twirled his glass, "…five hundred nicker at 100-to-8."

"That sounds near enough what a chap would need to establish a riding school," estimated Teddy.

"Could stretch to that." Oy nodded happily but was then struck by a cold, wet realisation. "But if Jimmy Fairly didn't lay off the bets, how is he going to cover the losses?"

"I expect he'll have to sell the Roller, at the very least, and might have to get by without a valet and mousseux made from hand-peeled grapes," speculated Teddy. "And if this puts him out of business, he could come and work for you in the Silver Ring, where you could keep an eye on him."

"He's welcome to my situation, if it suits you both, Mister Roy," proposed Chard. "I was thinking I'd take my winnings and shift operations to London, where a bloke and his dear old mum can get honest work."

"And how about you, Aunty?" asked Teddy. "Do you think you and the tea ladies will be able to manage without swindling punters?"

Aunty Azalea, huddled in her sandwich board like a tortoise with a warm whisky, affected to carefully consider the proposition before answering, softly and simply, "No."

"No? Fair enough. What about you, Vicar? Will today's winnings allow you to streamline church operations down to operating a church?"

"Oh, my heavenly choir, yes." Vicar Bittles shook his head in amazement, feeling just like the chap featuring in *On Jordan's Stormy Banks I Stand,* wondering how he got there. "I received the tips from Lady Bitterbrook and Lady Middleditch as generous guidance from a loving hand, of course, and not to be refused, but equally am I grateful for this bounty to relieve me of the anxiety of running an illicit gambling syndicate."

Teddy toasted a job well done and finished her whisky.

"I think that does it for the distribution of happy endings among the bookies and the bookers, and I expect the auction will be starting presently, Stilts. Let us go and enjoy the joint victory of Spoons and the Lady Lulu who loves him."

CHAPTER TWENTY

In which Spoons beats the odds, but Spoons doesn't.

"LLEWELLA'S TERRIBLY UPSET, TEDDY."

Markham Lord Middleditch intercepted Teddy and Stilts at the edge of the Tattersalls Enclosure to make this lolly-eyed announcement and, to press the point, hop on either foot and weave his fingers. On account of the rain, he'd kept his top hat on, much as he disliked it, and on account of the wind he'd tied it in place with his cravat. He wore his formal Wellingtons which were, in fact, appreciably muddier and more patched than his daily Wellingtons.

"What have you done, Uncle Bungle?"

"Nothing."

The Tattersalls Enclosure was a frenetic frisson of pother and fuss beneath a racked and towered canopy of umbrellas. Stilts led ahead like a flagship through and above the shifting sea of brollies and toppers.

"Why is Aunty Lew upset if you didn't do anything?" shouted Teddy over the crowd and rain.

"I told her that I didn't bid in the auction."

As he said this, the party arrived at the edge of the parade ground, roped into the centre of the enclosure. There they joined Lord and Lady Bitterbrook.

"Why did you tell her you didn't bid?" asked Teddy.

"She'd have noticed, eventually."

"No, I mean to say, what reason did you give her?"

"Ah." Markham posited that, by all appearances, as some sort of placeholder. That done, he briefly considered providing some sort of coherent answer to the question, but then got distracted by the rain.

"I advised him to not bid on Spoons," explained Lord Bitterbrook. "After a convincing win like that, against such long odds — it would draw some very unwanted attention from the stewards. Best if Markham maintains a low profile for the foreseeable, don't you think?"

"Fine. *I'll* bid on Spoons."

"Oh, dear, Teddy," sympathised Lady Bitterbrook. "I'm afraid it's too late."

The Tattersalls man, wearing grey swallowtails and topper and speaking in an Oxfordian honk, asked for quiet and didn't get it, but nevertheless announced the close of bidding.

In the same moment, Lady Llewella pushed through the crowd and in between Teddy and Lord Markham.

"Markham you must do something — I can't lose Spoons."

"He'll be much better cared for at Bitterbrook Stables, Llewella dear," Olivia assured her.

"Haa. Ha ha. Aaaah." Llewella mixed with a certain macabre talent a hollow laugh and a pout into the saddest social nicety ever heard at Bromford Bridge Racecourse.

The crowd applauded politely as the winner of the Bromford Bridge Easter Monday claim race for untried two-year-olds was led into the ring by an anxious stable lad who eyed the audience as though he suspected it of harbouring a sniper.

"What is *that?*"

This was posed by Lady Olivia in those very words and Lord Bitterbrook as the sound a debutant rugby player makes the first time he's sacked. Both were responding to the introduction of a brown and burgundy brindle-striped colt named Spoons.

"That's Spoons," Teddy helpfully provided. "That is Spoons, isn't it, Stilts?"

"Ehm…" Stilts leaned over the crowd. "Yes, that's Spoons."

"That's not Spoons," gogged Lady Olivia. "That's Pocket Change."

"Did you know, Lady Olivia," asked Teddy as casually as could be managed over the patter of the rain, "that a horse doesn't have a name, not officially at least, until he's registered for a sanctioned race?"

"But that's my horse," pointed out Lord Sticky. "I didn't register him for any race."

"I think you did, Sticks," differed Teddy. "I was right there when you signed the form."

"Form? What form? I signed no form."

"You did, Stickem, last night, in the library."

"Those were claim forms."

"Not all of them," explained Teddy. "It's been my experience, Stickles, that you must never sign anything with your real name unless you've read it very carefully." Teddy nodded sad sympathy at Lord Bitterbrook. "In fact, I feel quite sure that you did read the documents. Yes, yes I distinctly remember you putting on your pince-nez."

Lady Lulu blinked happy tears at Pocket Change. "Spoons didn't race?"

"He most certainly did race," Teddy assured her. "Came in a very respectable third, too. By the way, his name, officially, is Elmer's Bequest."

"We thought you'd appreciate that my dear," added Lord Markham. "We named him for the horse you had as a girl."

"Elmer's Bequest, you say," noted Lord Bitterbrook. "Perhaps my claim on him will be drawn."

"Do you have a claim on Elmer's Bequest?" asked Teddy.

"I have claims on all the horses. You know that — you gave me the documents to sign." Lord Bitterbrook settled a haughty eye on Teddy, and Teddy smiled simply as she waited for him to peel back the layers.

"You're not helping your uncle one bit, Teddy," claimed Lady Olivia. "Everyone's going to know that the jockey will have held back Spoons to only come in third."

"I rather think not, Lady Ols. Everyone who saw the race is going to say that Elmer's Bequest ran a sterling race considering his handicap."

"Handicap?" scoffed Sticky. "The maximum weight was ten pounds."

"I'm not referring to the added weight," specified Teddy. "I'm talking about wind resistance."

"Ah," twigged Lord Markham, who then whispered to Stilts, "She means his ears."

"Ehm, no, Your Lordship, I think Teddy means me," said Stilts. "I was riding Elmer's Bequest, if you'll recall." Stilts addressed the assembly to add, "Highlight of my year, I don't mind saying."

"You?" gogged Sticky. "You must be eight feet tall."

"Steady on, Your Lordship," irked Stilts. "You don't go about pointing out chaps with wooden legs, do you?"

"He probably does, though," noted, in passing, Teddy.

"Well, he shouldn't, is all I'm saying."

"He did his best," defended Teddy, "and so did Elmer's Bequest, and that's what matters to the stewards."

❧

"What matters to the stewards, Stanley, is that Markham has admitted cheating."

Lady Olivia and Lord Stanley Bitterbrook were in their tower suite at Middleditch, for a very brief exercise in packing when they next found themselves alone. Olivia, resigned to last week's Vionnet carnival gown designed for Lily Parr's proposed sitting for a portrait by Marie Laurencin, rang for Alice, and then opened her closets and scowled and the scant remains. Lord Sticky occupied himself with the careful selection and packing of stationery, toiletries, and what he suspected might be an antique bronze of 18th century undefeated stallion Flying Childers, but was in fact a souvenir paperweight.

"I can't believe I bought my own horse for a thousand pounds," lamented Lord Bitterbrook, as he carefully wrapped a gold-framed pen-and-ink of Ludlow racecourse in a pillow case. "And now Pocket Change is forever called 'Spoons'."

"At least he had a solid first race." Lady Olivia dropped a pair of Ferragamo sling-back pumps, designed for the opening of a second escalator at Harrods earlier that season, into the waste paper basket. "And we have the compensation of a hundred-to-8 win. How much did you bet, incidentally?"

"Bet? I didn't bet on Spoons. I bid on Spoons, I could hardly bet on him."

"Oh, Stanley!"

"Got to be mindful of appearances, my dear, a man in my position."

"Speaking of which, as you're so concerned with appearances, I'll thank you to be at your most wooden Westminster until we're shot of this marsh," warned Lady Olivia. "We'll have a civil farewell drink, then, regrettably, we must rush to catch our train, and once in London we'll go directly to the Jockey Club, where you can get Lord Markham and Middleditch Stables warned off forever."

CHAPTER TWENTY-ONE

Which finally reveals the secret of Chockit Rockit's burst of speed, the source of sadness in Spoons, the identity of a spy, and the recipe for the Nardo Lord Llannybidder Gin Gimlet.

"IT'S BEEN SUCH A DELIGHTFUL STAY, Llewella. I don't know how to thank you."

Lady Olivia issued this cavernously hollow platitude from the Bitterbrook side of the library at the stroke of cocktail hour.

"Ha ha ha," lied Lady Llewella, brazenly. On her drinking team was Lord Middleditch, Stilts, and Teddy, and Marshpool, who presently wheeled in the means of mixology. Teddy took up the tools. Little lines of rain bleared the windows, beyond which Middleditch racecourse glowed in a moonlit fog. In the stables, cosy and dry and victorious, Spoons and Chicken warmly approved of each other.

"Oh, I say, Lady O." Teddy clattered a handful of ice into the cocktail shaker. "I have an idea how you might thank your hosts — Lord Sticky can withdraw his objection with the Jockey Club. I'm so glad that's settled."

"I only wish I could," lamented Lord Sticky. "But Chockit Rockit's performance at Cheveley was, we can all agree, suspect. The Jockey Club needs to get to the bottom of it. You see, Teddy, this is just the sort of thing that can do the whole sport tremendous harm — it's a matter of appearances."

"Yes, I expect you're right, Lord Stickit." In the absence of lime juice and rigor, Teddy tipped an approximate too much cordial into the mixer "And, obviously, we'll stand by you."

"By me? I've nothing to do with it. It's not me that influenced Chockit Rockit with Scottish reels."

"Irish," corrected Markham.

"It wasn't Uncle Markham, either." Teddy drew out the moment with a slow pour of half a bottle of gin into the cocktail shaker before explaining, "The reason that Chockit Rockit performed poorly for five races before handily winning Cheveley is that it wasn't Chockit Rockit, it was a ringer. It was a horse called Overdraught."

"Overdraught is my horse," noted, with some little spirit, Lord Sticky.

"And as I say, we'll all stand by you." There was another pause while Teddy tambourined the cocktail mixer. "You probably didn't even know that Overdraught and Chockit Rockit had been swapped."

"They weren't swapped."

"That's the attitude, Stickles," Teddy encouraged. "But it's the only explanation — Chockit Rockit is a blur on the flat, except for five races at the beginning of the season when Pudge Hillock said that he was like a different horse."

"I don't think so Teddy," proceeded Lady Lewella with caution, "Chockit Rockit has very unique colouring."

"And so does Overdraught," pointed out Bitterbrook.

"And very pretty colouring it is, too, but it's not completely exclusive. In fact, I had a shimmy dress with a gold-speck effect like that, once, but I tore it shimmying down a drainpipe. You'd think, being a shimmy dress, it would have been better suited to task." Teddy apportioned a round of gin gimlets. "Have you ever seen Chockit Rockit, Lord Sticky?"

"I was in France for Cheveley."

"And have you ever seen Overdraught, Aunty Lu?"

"I don't think he's ever raced."

"You wouldn't know if you had." Teddy took up her gimlet. "Chockit Rockit and Overdraught are identical, owing to them being double cousins — their fathers are brothers and their mothers are sisters — but Chockit Rockit is fast on the flats and Overdraught is a gifted jumper. This is why they were both stabled here in Middleditch during the overlap of the National Hunt and Flat seasons, and this is how Mister Yardpole easily brought out the wrong horse for five races, until the end of jump season."

"Ah, but, Teddy..." Lord Middleditch, holding his gimlet in two hands and introducing it like newly discovered evidence, "...if all this is so, then to which horse was I playing Irish reels?"

"The point is, Uncle Mark, that it doesn't matter, Chockit Rockit was performing poorly because he wasn't Chockit Rockit, and when he returned to form it was because he was, once again, Chockit Rockit, and the Irish reels were just a very happy coincidence."

"The jockeys will have noticed, surely, Tedds," presumed Stilts.

"They would have, if they'd ever ridden both horses," replied Teddy. "But while Chockit Rockit was Overdraught, Flat Milliken was hiding out from what he assumed was a national arrest warrant. He only ever rode Chockit Rockit and Pudge Hillock only ever rode Overdraught."

"But how could Mister Yardpole make such a mistake?" wondered Lady Lew.

"I think you know the answer to that, Aunty L," levelled Teddy with a swirl of her gimlet. "When one season overlaps with another there are over two hundred horses stabled at Middleditch, and Mister Yardpole regularly mistakes some of them for horses that he last saw during the reign of Queen Victoria and, as you very well know, Lulu, he can't tell one chicken from another, either."

"I'm sure I don't know what you mean, Teddy."

"That's odd, because I'm sure that you do, Aunty," countered Teddy. "Spoons also performed poorly leading up to his first race, because you took away his chicken and replaced it with a ringer. You had Mister Yardpole unknowingly train a duplicate chicken to sit on Spoons' head, which is why Mister Yardpole said it felt like starting all over, sometimes."

"Swapping chickens?" Markham repeated the phrase as one mulling yet another of these inscrutable pastimes the youth of today are always inventing for themselves.

"Swapping chickens," confirmed Teddy. "Aunty Lulu was replacing the lookalike hen she'd acquired from the egg and poultry farm, not a mile down the road from the castle, and former home of Garibaldi, the early rising rooster. You see, she didn't want Spoons to race at all. Her plan, I expect, was to swap chickens at the beginning of each season so you'd postpone his maiden race until it was too late, and she and Spoons could ride forever through the fields of Shropshire. But then, when she learned that Spoons had to win the Bromford Bridge claim race or be put up for auction, she switched the chicken back."

"And that's why Her Ladyship was on the paddock late last night," twigged Stilts.

Teddy emptied the cocktail shaker into her glass and began a new composition, this time with more gin and less of everything else. ' Spoons was the subject of considerable espionage last night. Lady Llewella was there, as we now know, swapping chickens..."

"A much more difficult thing than one might think," recalled Lady Lulu. "Especially at night."

"And deftly done, too," lauded Teddy. "Just the way Raffles would have swapped a chicken, I expect, made particularly challenging by the Euston Station level of traffic the stable was seeing at the time; Aunty Azalea was gathering intelligence for her tout operation, Stilts just wanted his chance to ride a winner, and Marshpool..."

Marshpool, who had been happily subtracted from the main event and, as a further salve to his psyche, had been secretly drinking most of the day, started at the sound of his name introduced into conversation. Initially, he hoped it was a mistake — someone mispronouncing marzipan or March first, perhaps — but then after a moment's reflection he fell back on his pat defense. "No?"

"Marshpool was checking up on Spoons..." continued Teddy, mercilessly, "...in his capacity as Lord Bitterbook's spy at Middleditch Castle."

"No," Marshpool repeated his line, this time in an earnest, urgent pitch, like a man trying to stop a taxi, or time.

"Yes," corrected Teddy, and added a sort of exclamation mark in the form of a good shake of the cocktail mixer. "And this was after he thought I'd destroyed the letters with which Lord Sticky was blackmailing him."

"No... I... wait — *thought* you'd destroyed?"

"I suspected I might have use of them, and it turned out I was right. Stilts?"

Stilts withdrew a bundle of mismatched envelopes, bound in ribbon, from this breast pocket.

"Furthermore, Marshpool," Teddy received the envelopes and held them up for the court's perusal, "I know that it was you who told Lord Bitterbrook that Lord Markham won a fortune on Chockit Rockit at Cheveley."

A sad silence weighed upon the room. Finally Lord Markham, speaking tentatively, asked, "Oh, ehm, Marshpool... this spying business. It's not really done, is it?"

"Oh, I mean to say, well, yes, Your Lordship," ventured Marshpool. "Not in all great houses, of course, but in the main I'd say that most butlers function as agents of outside interests. In my last situation but one, the London residence of the, ehm, the Earl of Locksley, I was required to issue regular reports on the private movements of the household to *The Times.*"

"*The Times.*"

"And *The Mail,* with regards to matters of sport and haberdashery."

Once again, silence reigned. Marshpool tried looking dour and nodding contritely. Then he tried smiling and putting his hands in his pockets. Then he said, "I'll just pack my things, Your Lordship," and left the room.

"You might just as well have these back, Sticky." Teddy handed Bitterbrook the stack of letters.

Bitterbrook weighed the envelopes. "This can't be all of them."

"I've kept back some choice examples," explained Teddy. "There's a particularly ripe one on top, though, Sticks. Do have a look."

Bitterbrook, with a suspicious eye on Teddy, opened the topmost letter.

"It appears to promise Ruth, our parlour maid, devotion and a lifetime of shared bathing and..." The Bitterbrook eyebrows raised disapprovingly, "...frolics."

"What a lovely sentiment," said Teddy. "What do you make of the subscription?"

Lord Bitterbrook looked at the bottom of the letter, saw that it continued on the other side, turned it over, and read the signature...

'From Rupert Marshpool,
*   as dictated by Sticky Lord Bitterbrook.'*

Followed by the unmistakable signature of Stanley Lord Bitterbrook.

"I didn't write this."

"You signed it," Teddy pointed out to him. "You signed all of them, in fact."

"You tricked me — I thought I was signing claims forms."

"You rooked yourself, Sticks, by giving out as though you could read through Lady Brimble's pince-nez."

"Stanley, you gaping great ebb." Lady Olivia, apparently having reached and crossed by no small distance some sort of limit, stood up from her chair as though it had caught fire. "Very well. Teddy, Lord Bitterbrook will withdraw his objection with the Jockey Club. It will be a pleasure, in fact, an honour, because to do so we will finally have left this mouldering tower of damp." Olivia gestured about the library and then settled a bitterly ironic smile on Lord Markham, who smiled back. "And the lord of the marsh, the idiot savant, blunders once again to victory. He actually confessed to cheating and we still have to withdraw the objection. His absurd aviary destroyed his wife's garden. His terrible fiddle-playing — to make his horses run faster, if you will — nearly got his entire stable warned off for life, and his efforts to fix it nearly cost Llewella her ridiculous horse."

Lord Markham was born without the ability to take offense, and this handicap only grew more pronounced over the years. Now he simply smiled a baffled smile, and endeavoured to set the record straight, "It wasn't an aviary."

"It doesn't matter what it was," said Olivia. "It destroyed my entire wardrobe."

"It was a clubhouse, for Lulula and the chicken to watch Spoons train when it rained," explained Markham. "And I'd have never let Bitterbrook take Spoons away — I'd sooner be warned off for life than see Lulula unhappy."

Lady Olivia turned her awed despair on Lady Llewella. "I knew from the moment I met you at school, wearing your somehow simultaneously oversized and undersized uniform and tripping all over the hockey field, that you were going to marry some famous tangle and become an even greater laughing stock than you were then."

Lady Llewella, who had been laying down a solid foundation of nervous laughter, now ceased doing so. She set down her gin gimlet. She rose from her chair. She drew a breath that was somehow allusive to a trebuchet being armed. She loosed fire.

"What you mistake for dull-wittedness in my husband, Lady Olivia, is the soft edges of a kind heart. It's understandable you wouldn't recognise it, of course, having never inspired, earned, nor offered good will or amity, it only stands to reason that the qualities would strike you as foreign." Lady Lulu walked to the door, opened it, and stood aside. "And simply so you'll know where to direct your pointless ire, it wasn't Markham's blundering that flooded the ground floor, it was I, and it was deliberate. I did it for you, my dear old school chum, because I know how much you prize the acquisition of flimsy ephemera, and I wished to free up more space in your already vast, hollow existence. You're welcome."

❦

The rain pattered against the window of the library and the fire flickered in the fireplace. Teddy and Stilts tested the limits of gimlets and Lady Llewella reflected how much dash Lord Markham had retained from the day they were married.

"Fine bit of riding today, by the way, Stilts," commented Teddy. "Don't you think so, Unclers?"

"Eh?" Markham recovered from a Spoonsesque revery. "Oh, yes, well done, old man. Most expertly ridden."

"I expect you'll let Stilts course your horses during the training season, herewith," hinted Teddy.

"Oh, yes, of course. Most gladly."

"In spite of his height, I mean to say."

"Can't see that being much of a handicap during training."

"No, well, it's just you always refused to let him train in the past," Teddy reminded him.

"Ah, well, no, to be entirely accurate, Tedds, His Lordship didn't actually say I couldn't ride his horses, not in those words," clarified Stilts.

"You never asked, did you?" concluded, correctly, Teddy.

"Not as such."

"You just assumed you'd be refused, because you're tall."

"It is a presupposition which has served me well, in the main," replied Stilts coolly. "Reduces to a minimum disappointment and awkward situations."

"Perhaps Oy Roy will take you on as an instructor in his new riding school, too, if you'd only ask," suggested Teddy, shaking up a new recipe of gimlet, this time calling for gin, lemon zest, and gin.

"He's already proposed a summer retreat — Fielding for the Common Cack-Hander, he calls it," pronounced Stilts, and then translated "Jockeying for the clumsy, I think."

"I understand that Vicar Bittles has signed up the entire choir for riding lessons," inventoried Teddy. "Part of his plan to involve himself much more in church business, and only peripherally in the sport of kings."

"A lovely man," commented Lady Lulu, "but I expect I'll be seeing appreciably less of him in future."

"And perhaps more of Aunty Azalea, now that her tea ladies have decided to invest their winnings in pastry lessons and water-boiling facilities."

"How is your Aunt Azalea, dear?" asked Llewella. "I feel I haven't seen her in donkeys."

"She's been here a week," said Teddy. "She's in the north tower."

"The north tower is closed."

"That's why she's in the north tower," toasted Teddy with her gimlet. "You probably ran into her — did you encounter a pantomime horse or a temperance campaigner?"

"Yes, but I avoided them, obviously."

"And how did things work out for Jimmy Fairly, Stilts?" wondered Teddy.

"Much as you predicted — he and Somersby will be joining Oy's operation as leg men, if they can learn the local language," reported Stilts.

Everyone, with the exception of Lord Markham, sipped happily on their gimlets.

"All right, Uncler?" asked Teddy. "Not enough gin in your gin?"

"Quite frankly, Teddy, I'm preoccupied by poor Marshpool." Markham set aside his untouched gimlet, the better to pace the room. "I mean to say, it's not entirely his fault, the obligation under which he found himself."

"It most certainly is not," agreed Teddy. "After all, it wasn't him who told Lord Bitterbrook that you bet on Chockit Rockit."

"It wasn't?"

"Of course not. He had no call to. On the contrary — after I recovered the letters, his new loyalties were to the head office of Quillfeather and Quillfeather," said Teddy. "No, it was Lulu who grassed you up, Uncle Mark, because she was angry that you'd put Spoons up for a claim race."

Stilts and Markham slowly turned their surprised eyes on Lady Llewella.

"I'm afraid it's true," admitted Llewella. "I told Stanley that you asked me to bet on Chockit Rockit to win Cheveley. I'm dreadfully sorry, Markham — you were being such a top shelf bungler, but you've always been such a loveably top shelf bungler, I should have trusted you to bungle things out nicely in the end."

Lord Markham brooded on this or, possibly, on a stain on the floor. It was difficult to tell from his expression or point of focus. Finally, this effort produced results, "But you said that it was Marshpool."

"I did," conceded Teddy. "At the time, I had need for Lady Olivia to believe that she still had poor Marshpool under her thumb." Teddy tasted her gimlet and then held it to the light with a dissatisfied air. "You know what this needs, Stilts, to make it a proper Nardo Lord Llannybidder Gimlet?"

"More gin?" guessed Stilts.

"Please. Just ring for another bottle, will you?"

Stilts gave the bellpull a double tuggle and, within a moment Marshpool came through the door.

"You rang, sir?" he asked Lord Markham.

Lord Markham blinked happily at the prodigal butler and he, too, wondered if he rang.

"I did, Marshlands," said Teddy. "Did you see Lord and Lady Bitterbrook off all right?"

"Yes, Miss," replied Marshpool. "Her Ladyship was most grateful for the information."

"I'm so glad. It would have been unkind to let them leave empty-handed."

❦

East Mosley in Surrey, some twenty pleasant miles from London, is a handy, happy suburb characterised by a bustling high street, numerous and extensive green parks, a democratically broad spectrum of fully detached, attached, and apartment dwellings, convenient transport links, and foot access to Hampton Court Palace, just across the river.

Pleasant as it is, the day following the Bromford Bridge Easter Monday races was the first time that Lady Olivia Bitterbook had ever been or ever considered going to East Mosley. Nevertheless, there she was, being released from her Bentley by her driver in front of the one East Mosley institution in which she had found an interest, the Imber Court stables.

Little space is wasted at the efficient Imber Court, and in the front yard there was a sort of obstacle course at which Lady Olivia stood and marvelled. These constantly changing, untried and improbable training methods were something of a bête noir for the traditionalist, who liked to see her horses train for racing by racing This was nothing of the kind. At Imber Court that day, a stoic black mare with an oversized jockey was marching with poise and precision while, all about her, men in cloth caps harassed her with all manner of distraction, including protest signs, flags, smoke pots and, in one extreme case, a set of cymbals.

A note of explanation would have set her mind to rest — this racing regime only seemed odd because it was nothing of the sort. The unflappable mare was training for a role in crowd control, because Imber Court stables is a stabling and training ground for police horses, and all the men in cloth caps were constables.

"Young man," beckoned Lady Olivia to the chap with the cymbals. 'Please stop that and come over here. I wish to speak to the man in charge."

"Can I help you miss?" said the constable in what would have been to, say, Teddy, a tellingly constabulary fashion.

"I have business to discuss with the management here," announced Lady Olivia, "and I'm very pressed for time. I'm catching the boat train to Paris in less than an hour."

"Business, madam?"

"Yes. Business, regarding Piccadilly Larking. My name is Tilly Fivequidder."

Teddy Quillfeather Mysteries

Thank you for reading *Frauds On Favourite*, the most multi-layered, multi-played, *mille-feuille* farce yet to convolute the Quillfeather canon.

I hope the multiple mini-mysteries, subplots, subterfuge, subtexts, and pretexts overlapped in a manner that made them only just difficult enough to work out for those who wanted to, and resulted in a fast-paced first-placed mystery either way.

You'll have noticed that there's rather a lot of Cockney, Mockney, and equestrian and bookmaking jargon and practice in *Frauds on Favourite*. I did more research for this book than any other and the result, I think, is just enough expertise to be certain that I got any number of details wrong. That's my fault, though, and not that of my sources, such as several racing mysteries by Dick Francis — *Come to Grief* (Michael Joseph, 1995), *Whip Hand* (Michael Joseph, 1979), *Under Orders* (Penguin, 2006), and *Odds Against* (Penguin, 1965). I gathered rather a lot of matter from Francis' stories along with an admiration for the easy manner in which he presents it.

I also read an entire dictionary: *The Language of Horse Racing*, by Gerald Hammond (Routledge, 2000), which, for a dictionary and, for that matter, any reference book, is a very entertaining read.

Talking of entertaining reads, if you enjoyed *Frauds on Favourite*, odds are you'll like some of the following titles...

Hardy Haul at Hardy Hall

In which timing is everything, all hope is lost for the next generation, a burglary is announced, and Teddy Quillfeather prepares for what promises to be a challenging away derby.

The theft of an immensely valuable, immensely ugly necklace is only the beginning of the intrigues and oddities at a country weekend at Hardy Hall where Teddy Quillfeather's mother has sent her with strict instructions to select an eligible bachelor from a shortlist of aristocrats, eccentrics, and egos.

But when Teddy sets out to discourage the suitors and discover the looters with her natural knack for applied shenanigans she instead uncovers countless conspiracies, complicated by country house courtesies. It's a comedy of manners and caper of manors and the only solution, if you're Teddy Quillfeather, is obviously another heist.

Frauds On Favourite

In which the reader is introduced to practical Cockney, and the only way to guaranteed way to be first past the post.

Teddy's off to the races in this multi-layered multiplier mystery of dark horses and dodgy courses, pawky jockeys, unstable stables, impossible odds, crooked bookies, and a track-wide conspiracy to deny the punter an even chance. That's more than enough to invite a counter-con from Teddy, but when the family paddock is implicated in race-fixing, she does what she does best when the odds go against her — she raises the stakes.

Monet for Nothing

In which Teddy visits Paris for a clash of culture, a splash of wine, and a dash of casual smuggling.

Taking refuge from London's mating season among the posers, poets, and painters of Montmartre, Teddy's soon at the centre of the impossible heist of a priceless masterpiece on its way to auction.

Teddy's friends are under the gavel as the auction approaches but what's a girl to do when the clues split in two and mysteries multiply? Teddy's talent for the art of the artifice is on display as she connects the dots, makes an impression, and colours outside the lines.

Anty Boisjoly Mysteries

Teddy's cousin Anty Boisjoly is a golden-age gad and fun-loving lad who approaches all things with a happy enthusiasm that he endeavours to render contagious. His talent for twisty mystery suits him well as every stand-alone, self-contained story is guaranteed to have two locked room murders plus multiple subplots and lashings of eccentric suspects.

The Case of the Canterfell Codicil

Featuring The Suspicious Circumstance of the Sealed Study, The Main Course Mystery, and The Puzzling Case of the Puzzling Case
In *The Case of the Canterfell Codicil*, Wodehousian gadabout and clubman Anty Boisjoly takes on his first case when his old Oxford chum and coxswain is facing the gallows, accused of the murder of his wealthy uncle. Not one but two locked-room mysteries later, Anty's matching wits and witticisms with a subversive butler, a senile footman, a single-minded detective-inspector, an irascible goat, and the eccentric conventions of the pastoral Sussex countryside to untangle a multi-layered mystery of secret bequests, ancient writs, love triangles, revenge, and a teasing twist in the final paragraph.

The Case of the Ghost of Christmas Morning

The Final Flight of Flaps Fleming
Anty Boisjoly visits Aunty Boisjoly, his reclusive aunt, at her cosy, sixteen-bedroom burrow in snowy Hertfordshire, for a quiet Christmas in dairy country. But even before he arrives, a local war hero has not only been murdered in a most improbable fashion, but hours later he's standing his old friends Christmas drinks at the local.

The only clues are footprints in the snow, leading to the only possible culprit — Aunty Boisjoly.

The Tale of the Tenpenny Tontine

The dual duel dilemma
It's another mystifying, manor house murder for bon-vivant and problem-solver Anty Boisjoly, when his clubmate asks him to

determine who died first after a duel is fought in a locked room. The untold riches of the Tenpenny Tontine are in the balance, but the stakes only get higher when Anty determines that, duel or not, this was a case of murder.

The Case of the Carnaby Castle Curse
The Brisk Business of Being Boisjoly
The ancient curse of Carnaby Castle has begun taking victims again — either that, or someone's very cleverly done away with the new young bride of the philandering family patriarch, and the chief suspect is none other than Carnaby, London's finest club steward.

Anty Boisjoly's wits and witticisms are tested to their frozen limit as he sifts the superstitions, suspicions, and age-old schisms of the mediaeval Peak District village of Hoy to sort out how it was done before the curse can claim Carnaby himself.

Reckoning at the Riviera Royale
A Menacing Beckoning to an Unsettling Reckoning
Anty finally has that awkward 'did you murder my father' conversation with his mother while finding himself in the ticklish position of defending her and an innocent elephant against charges of impossible murder.

If that's not enough, Anty's fallen for the daughter of the mysterious mother-daughter team of gamblers, there's a second impossible murder, and Anty has a very worrying idea who it is that's been cheating the casino.

The Case of the Case of Kilcladdich
Will a Still Still Still Still?
Anty Boisjoly travels to the sacred source waters of Glen Glennegie to help decide the fate of his favourite whisky, but an impossible locked room murder is only one of a multitude of mysteries that try Anty's wits and witticisms to their northern limit.

Time trickles down on the traditional tipple as Anty unravels family feuds, ruptured romance, shepherdless sheep, and a series of suspiciously surfacing secrets to sort out who killed whom and how and why and who might be next to die.

Foreboding Foretelling at Ficklehouse Felling
The Medium with the Message of the Most Perilous of Presage

It's a classic, manor house, mystery-within-a-locked-room-mystery for Anty Boisjoly, when a death is foretold by a mystic that Anty's sure is a charlatan. But when an impossible murder follows the foretelling, Anty and his old ally and nemesis Inspector Wittersham must sift the connivance, contrivance, misguidance, and reliance on pseudoscience of the mad manor and its oddball inhabitants before the killer strikes again.

Mystery and Malice Aboard RMS Ballast
Tales of Sails and Betrayals and for Some Reason Mails

Anty, Vickers, Inspector Wittersham, and a passenger list of howling eccentrics find themselves prey to the sway and spray of the Scilly Seas when what at first seems a simple, unexplainable, locked-state-room murder twists into a tale of buried treasure, perilous weather and dangerous endeavours at sea.

Death Reports to a Health Resort
Imposters and Spices and the Virtues of Vices

We meet more of Anty's eccentric extended family when he visits his uncle at a retreat for fans of the first deadly sin and enthusiasts of the sixth. Motivated suspects are plump, piqued, and plentiful when the most disliked man in the spa is the victim of a locked room murder, but Inspector Wittersham soon points the finger at Anty's uncle and things only get worse when a second murder occurs that both eye-witnesses — Anty Boisjoly and Ivor Wittersham — swear was impossible.

The False Clue of the Twisted Red Herring's Footprint
The tenth Anty Boisjoly Mystery!

It's the biggest Boisjoly by bounds when none other than Anty's friendly rival Inspector Wittersham is the only suspect in a locked-room murder.

Of course Anty doesn't believe for a second that Inspector Wittersham murdered a prisoner locked in a cell to which only he had the key, it's merely unfortunate that the more Anty investigates and the more twists and secrets and hidden treasure he digs up, the more evidence he finds that proves Wittersham guilty.

To save his friend, Anty must draw on his judgemental mum, woolly valet, multitude members of the Juniper Gentleman's Club, his own depths of wit and anecdote, and endless eccentrics as he delves deeply into the history of medieval England and the Boisjoly family's dark past.

The next one!

It seems that Anty and Teddy are always being drawn into mystery and intrigue. If you'd like to receive warning of the next locked room murder, heist, swindle, stratagem, or sting, along with cryptic clues and custom content and cartoons, you can subscribe the combined Boisjoly/Quillfeather Intermittent Newsletter at the link below or by flashing the QR code on your phone.

http://indefensiblepublishing.com/newsletters/

Printed in Dunstable, United Kingdom